To Michael
Enjoy th

The Wizard of Balalac

The Wizard of Balalac

From The Book of Mysteries

by Fran Orenstein

The Wizard of Balalac
From the Book of Mysteries

Sleepytown Press
1709 Valley Creek Road
Anniston, Alabama 36207

Cover design by Randy Young

Second edition printed in North America

ISBN: 978-0-9826344-2-4

Printed in the U.S.A.
February 2010

"The Magician Merlin…" from World Of Wonders [1976] A Bottle in the Smoke by Robertson Davies

This book is dedicated to the special children in my life

Rachel Claire
Aaron Alexander
Zayden Miles
Vaughn Michael
and
children everywhere who love books Read On!

A special thank you to

Susannah Orenstein for excellence in editing

Artist, author and publisher, Randy Young for the great cover, infinite patience and technical assistance
www.sleepytownpress.weebly.com

and

Deborah Simpson, poet, author and seer, whose on-going support, advice, and patience made this possible www.deborahsimpson.org

The author may be contacted at
www.franorenstein.weebly.com

Coming in 2010 from Fran Orenstein

The Gargoyles of Blackthorne
From the Book of Mysteries

The Mystery Under Third Base
A Huby Mystery

The Goblin Murder Mystery
A Huby Mystery

Chapter 1

Uncle Tad's Secret

“It’s time. Yes, it’s definitely time,” the tall, thin man muttered to himself.

Tyler Trent sat frozen in the chair. Only his eyeballs moved as he watched his uncle pace back and forth. Sometimes, Thaddeus Trent would stop and stare at Tyler, shake his head, and then continue pacing. Tyler jumped when Uncle Tad clapped his hands together and shouted, “By God, it is most definitely time!” Then he put his big nose two inches from Tyler’s smaller nose and asked, “Twelve years old?”

Tyler moved his head slightly, afraid to shake it too hard and bump into Uncle Tad’s face.

Thaddeus backed up. "Excellent age. Perfect for your first adventure."

Tyler warmed very fast. Uncle Tad's idea of an adventure was being chased out of the Amazon jungle by a tribe of headhunters or nearly being mauled by a twelve-foot bear in Alaska. Tomorrow he was leaving for some unpronounceable island in the middle of the Pacific Ocean to dive for sunken ships. He would probably be electrocuted by a giant eel.

In spite of his flopping stomach, Tyler asked in a squeaky voice, "Uh, what kind of adventure, Uncle Tad?"

"Ahh, glad you asked. You must find a shop called Beadlesberry's Rare Books. That in itself is difficult because the bookshop is sometimes there and sometimes not," Thaddeus said.

Tyler squinted up at his uncle. "What?"

Thaddeus smirked. "Well sometimes it disappears. Let's just say, it's an unusual bookstore."

Tyler nodded like he knew what his uncle was talking about.

"Good boy," Thaddeus said. "I knew you would understand. There's a lot of me in you, in spite of your parents."

Tyler shuddered to think he was anything like Uncle Tad, but he was too polite to say anything.

"Now where was I?" Thaddeus said, scratching his ear. "Of course. First you find the bookstore, 76th and 6th. Take the uptown bus to 75th and then walk one block north. It's on the left, if it's there. Or was it the right? No, I distinctly remember the left, between the candy store and the drugstore. The book you want is called The Book of Mysteries. Great fun. And watch that Beadlesberry. Strange fellow, really strange." Thaddeus flicked his wrist toward his face. "Oops, I'm late. Have to catch that flight west. You enjoy your adventures, and be sure to tell me all about it when I see you again." He spun toward the door, took two giant strides, stopped, and twisted around. "Make friends with the book or it will thwart all your fun."

"Wait, Uncle Tad," Tyler cried, but his uncle was gone with a breezy slam of the door. Tyler shook his head. What was that all about? Like he would really go look for a disappearing bookstore. What did thwart mean?

He wanted to tell somebody about the book. He wished Zack were around to talk to. Best friends were supposed to be there when you needed them, not off visiting relatives. Then he remembered that it was Friday and Zack would be back tonight and probably ready to get into trouble as usual.

Tyler figured Zack would think it was fun to take the bus uptown and look for an invisible bookstore. They could say they were going to a bookstore. There were enough of them in Manhattan. Books and school were magic words to Mom. It would only take a couple of hours. Maybe if he said he was looking for a special book but didn’t say where, well, it wasn’t really lying. More like leaving out. Tyler shook his head. All this thinking would give him a headache.

What if the bookstore was in its disappearing mode and he couldn't find it? He couldn't keep going back to look for it. Tyler smacked his head and mumbled to no one in particular. "You sound as nuts as Uncle Tad. There's no such thing as a disappearing bookstore anyway." Or was there? Tyler giggled nervously. No rush, he'd decide after he talked it over with Zack.

He opened the door and sniffed the air. Chocolate chip cookies. Tyler tiptoed into the kitchen and crept past his mother's back toward the counter. She whirled around. "I see you, Tyler Trent. Don't you dare, they just came out

of the oven."

Tyler threw up his hands. There had to be a third eye someplace under all that hair. "Okay, okay. Uncle Tad just left."

"Yes, thank God. I can't believe your father could have a brother like Thaddeus. Always getting into trouble, even as a boy." She peered closely at Tyler. "At least you're like your father, sane."

Tyler giggled. His father Tiberius Trent was a professor of archeology at the university. He dreamed all year of the next archeological dig so he could drag the family to broil in the heat of the desert and freeze in arctic just to turn up a bone or two. He was so absentminded he needed a map to find the bathroom.

"What is so funny?" his mother asked.

"Nothing, Mom. What does thwart mean?"

His mother wrinkled her forehead. "Prevent something from happening. I wish your father and I could thwart your Uncle's plans."

Tyler nodded. His mother, the English professor, always knew the answers. "Thanks. Zack's coming home tonight. Are we doing anything important tomorrow? I thought maybe Zack and me could go, um, look for this book I need for history."

"Zack and I." His mother smiled and reached out to touch his cheek. "Ah yes, a reader just like me. Come give your Mom a hug."

Tyler was swept into his mother's soft arms. He would never admit it, but he still liked the warm feel of her body and the soapy smell of her skin. He thought his mother was pretty with her soft brown hair and blue eyes. She was short and plump, not all bony like Zack's mother. She was a just right mother. Then she pushed him back and smoothed a brown curl off his face. "You need a haircut, young man. Cookies after dinner."

"Yes!" Tyler said as he ran to his room. Arms outstretched, he whirled around and around. "Tomorrow the bookstore, maybe."

Tyler looked in the mirror. He saw a smaller version of Uncle Tad, and of course his father. Uncle Tad was his father's younger brother and they looked exactly alike. Long face, long nose and squinty brown eyes. Tyler was already taller than most of his friends, with a nose that seemed to grow daily and out-of-control brown hair.

Uncle Tad always dressed in black. He said it was good camouflage, except of course in snow country where he wore all white. Uncle Tad was so cool. He always had an exciting story to tell and he never ruffled Tyler's hair or tried to give him wet kisses. Tyler's mother said Thaddeus was an adventurer and was lucky he was still alive. She was afraid that one day Thaddeus would find himself in a situation he could not escape; like getting eaten by a lion in Africa or falling off a mountain in Tibet. He always came back, though, with another tale scary enough to freeze your blood.

Tyler came from a family of adventurers, except his mother. Her greatest adventure was surviving another day teaching a college freshman English class. She once announced, laughing, "Those kids wouldn't know Shakespeare if I hit them over the head with a volume of his greatest works. But, it might wake them up."

Chapter 2

To Go or Not To Go

Dinner dragged on and on. Tyler jiggled his leg so hard water slopped over the glasses. "Tyler, stop that," His mother said. "What is wrong with you tonight? You're jumpier than a grasshopper."

"What grasshopper? Madeleine, did you candy grasshoppers for desert? Remember the time we ate them in South America. Quite tasty." His father grinned. "Although, I do recall that you were not very happy once you found out what they were."

His mother laughed. "No dear, there are only chocolate chip cookies tonight."

Tyler swallowed hard. Appetite gone, he pushed the fork around his plate, rearranging the food. "Grasshoppers for desert," he mumbled. "Yuck, gross, disgusting."

"Did you say something, Tyler?" his mother asked.

Tyler shook his head. He barely listened to his father ramble on non-stop about an exciting fossil discovery in Arizona, and that maybe they would stay in the United States this year instead of running off to some desert in the Middle East. His mother just nodded and smiled. Tyler could only think about Uncle Tad and the disappearing bookstore. Finally, his father wound down and went off to his study. Tyler helped his mother clear the table, but when he nearly dropped the water pitcher she sent him out of the kitchen.

Tyler paced back and forth in the hallway, watching the elevator. The hands on his watch never seemed to move. Finally, the light went on and the elevator crept up to the seventh floor. Tyler stood against the wall facing the elevator.

The doors slid open and Zack stepped out, followed by his ten-year-old sister, Carrie. "Hi Tyler," she crowed. "Did you miss me?"

Tyler tried not to laugh. "Sure, Carrie, like I miss a case of poison ivy."

Carrie marched off, chin up in the air.

"Hello, Tyler," Mrs. Vander said, pushing hair off her face. "I'm exhausted. Please tell your mother I'll come over tomorrow."

Mr. Vander appeared next. "Hello Tyler, figured you'd be waiting right here all night until we got home."

"Hello, Mr. Vander," Tyler said. "Can Zack come over for a few minutes?"

"I guess," he said. "You probably had withdrawal symptoms from being apart an entire week."

Tyler and Zack looked at each other "What are withdrawal symptoms?" Tyler whispered.

Zack shrugged. "I think it's something you get when you stop taking drugs."

Tyler yanked his friend down the hall. "Never mind. Come on, I have to tell you something."

The boys ran to Tyler's room. "Tyler is that you?" His mother called.

"Yes, Mom. Zack is back."

Mrs. Trent appeared in the doorway holding a plate of cookies. "Hello, Zack. Did you have a nice time?"

Zack stopped short and stared at the cookies. "I guess." He licked his lips.

Mrs. Trent held out the plate to Zack. "Chocolate Chip."

"I missed your cookies, thanks. Oh, and my Mom says she'll be over tomorrow." Zack took the plate and followed Tyler down the hall.

They sat on the floor and Zack stuffed cookies into his mouth as Tyler told him about Uncle Tad and the disappearing bookstore. He watched Zack's green eyes light up and a big grin stretch his freckles.

"Cool, a bookstore that vanishes and then reappears. This I've got to see. So when are we going?" Zack asked, barely able to sit still.

Tyler shrugged. "Yeah, well, what if it disappears while we're inside?"

"Come on, you don't really believe a building can disappear and reappear, do you?" Zack asked.

"How should I know? So answer my question. What happens to us?"

It was Zack's turn to shrug. "Scientifically, it can't happen, okay? So stop worrying so much. You're starting to sound like my mother."

Tyler grinned, "Not that, please."

Zack laughed. “Okay, so like I said, when are we going?”

A cold shiver ran down his back, and Tyler made his decision. “How about tomorrow? I already told my mom I needed a book for history.”

“Okay, you’re on.” Zack yawned. “I'm going home. See you in the morning."

After Zack left, Tyler lay on his bed staring at the ceiling. “Maybe this is a stupid idea after all,” he muttered. Suddenly a cape of darkness enveloped the room and Tyler shivered. Glancing at the blackness outside the window, Tyler thought, ‘It got dark awfully fast tonight. Maybe a storm is coming.’ He switched on the table lamp flooding the room with light. Tyler got out the latest Harry Potter book, and settled down to read.

Chapter 3

The Keeper of the Books

As soon as he stepped off the bus, Tyler knew this was a big mistake. Black clouds threatened overhead. Cold fingers of electric-tinged air tickled the back of his neck. He shuddered and rubbed his skin as he waited for Zack to catch up. They walked north and then turned the corner. The bookstore was visible today. Tyler shook his head. That was stupid. A store was either there or not there. It didn't just come and go whenever it felt like it. From where he stood, he could see the wooden sign swinging in the increasing wind, BEADLESBERRY'S RARE BOOKS. An eerie glow spread beneath the dark clouds. Thunder rumbled in the distance.

Zack poked a finger in his back. "I guess that's the bookstore."

Tyler jumped.

Zack laughed. "Sorry, I didn't mean to scare you."

Tyler said, "You didn't scare me." He looked back the way they had come. There was still time to change his mind. "Maybe we should come back Monday, after school."

"No way," Zack said taking off down the street. Then Tyler clenched his fists and hurried after him. It was always easier to be brave with your best friend. Maybe they could still beat the storm if the book he wanted was on the shelf.

The boys stopped short in front of the shop. A hand-lettered sign hung in the glass-fronted door "WE CLOSE FOR STORMS." The lights were out inside the shop. Tyler cupped his hands along his face and peered in the window. He couldn't see anything in the blackness. Suddenly a candle flickered and a white oval appeared an inch from his eyes. Tyler jumped back, the beat of a bass guitar thumping in his chest. "Did you see that?" he yelled. An entire heavy metal rock band was where his heart should have been. The banging rose to his head and down to his toes.

"See what?" Zack asked, putting his face against the door. A crack of thunder masked the click of the door. A claw snaked out and snared his wrist, pulling him through the doorway. Zack yelped, struggling to free his wrist. Another cold claw pulled Tyler inside, and the door slammed shut behind them.

"Relax, young masters, I won't eat you, already had my lunch. Besides I don't favor eating 12 year-old boys, too tough. Girls now…hmm, a little sweeter. Yet, sometimes they're tough too, but stewed well with mushrooms and onions, girl stew might be tasty." The voice cackled and ended in a coughing fit.

The pressure on his wrist lifted, and Tyler backed up, hitting the door and rattling the glass. He couldn't breathe.

"Hey there, are you alright? I surely didn't mean to scare you like that, Tyler," the dark figuresaid. The candle moved closer and a bony old man dressed entirely in black came into focus behind the flickering light.

Tyler pressed harder into the glass door. He still couldn't breathe, but his head bobbed up and down. The old man's eyes glowed like black marbles in the firelight and his white hair fell down around his shoulders.

"Good." The old man's lips curled up under his jagged, pointy nose, one side of his mouth higher than the other. "I wouldn't want to lose the only customers of the day. Just let me get some more light in here. Have to watch the candles, books burn you know," he laughed, his voice cracking.

Tyler could hear Zack breathing hard beside him. He could see the room now. Bookcases soared to the ceiling. Piles of books covered every available surface. He sneezed.

"Ah good, you're breathing again, Tyler." The old man was standing behind him.

The old man pointed a bony finger at his jacket. "Says so right there in big white letters, Tyler. So unless you stole it, that's your name."

Tyler glanced down at his name. Okay, but it only made sense if the old man could see in the dark. Better not to ask that question.

Then the old man turned to Zack. "You, Zachary, are you breathing too?"

Zack's voice squeaked. "I'm not wearing a jacket. How do you know my name?"

The old man just tapped his head. "So, brave lads, you came here for the book?"

Tyler frowned. Did the old man say 'the' book, like he knew what book they wanted? "How do you know where anything is? Nothing is marked," Tyler asked.

The old man grinned, a lopsided grin of brown, crooked teeth. "Good question, smart young man. I know where everything is." Then he pointed, spinning around. "Nature, spells, mysteries, adventure, witchcraft, plays, poetry, travel, magic." He stopped in front of a high bookcase. "This is what you came here to find." He stood on his tiptoes and reached up, pulling down a thin, brown book. "Take it smart young man, don't be shy."

Thunder rolled overhead and the first drops of rain splattered the window. Tyler reached out for the book. It vibrated in his hand and he almost dropped it.

"Careful now, young Tyler Trent, you don't want to drop that book."

Tyler remembered his Uncle's warning to stay on the good side of the book. He couldn't believe he just thought of that. A book was just paper and ink. Just to be sure, he carefully turned the book over and held it near the candle. Fat gold letters said The Book of Mysteries. He turned to the old man. "Who are you? How could you know what book I was looking for? And how did you know my last name, it's not on my jacket. How did you know Zack's name? How did you know how old we are? I've never met you before. I've never even been in this store."

The old man grinned crookedly. "You ask too many questions, nosy boy. I know lots of things, young Tyler. It's my job to know. I'm the keeper of the books, Bartholomew B. Beadlesberry, bookseller and know-it-all at your service." He bowed stiffly.

Tyler turned to Zack, but he was still frozen against the door. "This is too weird," Tyler said, backing towards his friend. "Uh, how much is the book? We really have to get home."

"It's not for sale," the old man said firmly.

"What are you talking about? This is a bookstore, isn't it? I mean you sell books here, don't you?" Tyler gritted his teeth. First they had to take a bus, then walk for blocks and outrun a storm, and now the old man wouldn't sell the book.

Zack grabbed his arm, pulling him toward the door. "Never mind the book, let's get out of here," he whispered frantically.

The old man's eyes opened wide. "Some books are for sale and some aren't. Besides, you can't just buy this book and go home. What if you opened it and said the wrong things, then you might find yourself in a cave facing Tyrannosaurus Rex."

Rain rapped like machine guns against the window. Glancing over his shoulder at the door, Tyler said, "It's just a book of stories. I'm not going to end up in some cave somewhere a million years ago."

"Don't be sure, brave Tyler. The last person who owned this book disappeared into tenth-century Wales, or was it ninth-century Scotland, probably burned alive by a fiery dragon. Tell me, boy, how did you learn about the book? "

Tyler shuddered. "My uncle told me about it."

"Your uncle? Of course," The old man said, scratching his head. "Trent, Thaddeus Trent. I should have known from the brown curly hair and those dark brown eyes. You look like him, even got his dimple in your chin. Of course, your nose is smaller. He was just about your age when he first came here. Couldn't get enough of the adventures. Where did he go? Let me think a minute. It's been a long time. I don't remember so well anymore."

Tyler didn't believe that for a minute. This old guy remembered everything and knew things he couldn't possibly know. Thunder boomed right overhead and a flash of lightening lit up the room. Tyler jumped. The old man cackled. "Scared you, didn't it?"

Tyler stood up straight. "I'm not scared," he said. The old man was just trying to shock him and the storm didn't make him feel any better. It was impossible that the old man could know Uncle Tad's name and what he looked like. Tyler peered out the window, but the rain blocked his view. There was another blast of thunder followed in a few seconds by a streak of lightening. Tyler knew the storm would move off soon. Maybe he could just humor the old man and hold out a little bit longer.

The old man squawked, "I remember, Thaddeus Trent went to Camelot. Served as a page to Sir Lancelot, I believe. Had a very exciting adventure, even met Merlin, greatest magician of all ages. That was a time of masterful magic." The old man opened his hand and shook out a huge black and white striped handkerchief and wiped a tear from his cheek. He blew his nose loudly and the handkerchief disappeared. Then he leaned toward the boys and recited in a loud voice, waving his hands dramatically, "The magician Merlin had a strange laugh, and it was heard when nobody else was laughing....He laughed because he knew what was coming next." The old man's grin carved a slit across his face, his cackle mingling with a clap of thunder.

Tyler blinked, the book trembling in his hand. What did that mean and where did the handkerchief go? "Okay, suppose you're right. Does that mean the book will let me travel to the past?" Then he shook his head. "This is dumb. It's just not physically possible to travel in time, especially not through a book. It's just paper and ink."

The old man eyes glittered. "Anything is possible, Tyler the unbeliever. You can travel to the past or even to the future. You just have to believe in magic. Your Uncle Thaddeus believed." Then he turned to Zack. "Your friend Zack believes, don't you boy?"

Zack had stopped shaking. He thought for a moment. "I don't really know. I mean there are strange things that happen in the world. I guess it's possible."

Beadlesberry nodded happily. "Smart answer, clever Zachary."

Tyler was convinced the old man was crazy. All he had to do was stick it out for 10 or 15 minutes and he would get out of this place. "Listen, suppose I pay you now for the book." Tyler reached into his pocket.

The old man turned his back. "The boy just won't listen," he muttered to nothing in particular. Then he hobbled over to a table and pushed aside a stack of books. Clearing some more books off a chair, he lowered his body slowly, bony legs and chair legs creaking together. He patted the back of the other chair. "Come here, brave Tyler, and bring the book." Then he looked at Zack and waggled his finger. "And you, Zachary, the believer."

Tyler wasn't feeling very brave; he just wanted to get out of here. Once more, thunder rolled over the shop and golden fingers of lightening flashed outside.

Chapter 4

The Book of Mysteries

Zack leaned toward Tyler and whispered, "Listen, we can't leave now, it's raining too hard. Let's just sit down until the storm stops. The old man can't force us to do anything we don't want to do, right?"

Tyler reluctantly walked to the table, Zack following close behind. They moved piles of books off the chairs and sat down, Tyler still clutching the book to his chest.

"Well, put the book down here on the table, Tyler Trent. Somebody would think you got impaled by a sliver of lightening, way you're acting."

Tyler laid the book on the table and rubbed his hands together. His fingers were icy cold.

"That's better Tyler. You have to be a boy who pays attention if you want to read this book."

Tyler glared at the old man. "I thought you said it wasn't for sale."

The old man poked his finger into Tyler's chest. "None of your sass, boy. I said it's not for sale, I didn't say you couldn't read it right here."

Now Tyler was thoroughly confused. Did the old man really expect him to come down here every day to read the book? "Mr. Beadlesberry, I'm sorry you don't want to sell the book, but I can't come here to read it, it's just too far from my apartment. Let's just forget we ever came here. We'll just wait at the door for the storm to pass and then we'll be out of your way." Tyler stood up, but the old man pulled him back down.

"You're going to be sorry you missed the adventure of a lifetime, young Tyler Trent. This book can take you anywhere you want to go, to the future, the past, or any magical world you choose. You too, young Zachary." The old man's eyes sparkled.

Tyler opened his mouth to speak but a loud clap of thunder drowned out all sound.

"Indeed, indeed," said Beadlesberry. "Absolutely right. I haven't given you enough information."

Tyler shrank back and glanced at Zack, who shrugged. How could the old man know what he was going to say before the clap of thunder? It was getting spookier by the second. Tyler made a decision. He would just sit here and not move or make a sound. The minute the storm passed, he would run as fast as he could and never come back.

"Now, pay attention, terrified Tyler. You too, Zachary." Tyler felt Zack's body jerk upright. The old man flipped the book over. "This book has two covers. One side goes to real time and the other side goes to magic time. Following me so far, boys?"

Tyler nodded, afraid to speak. "Good. Now watch." Beadlesberry opened the back cover to the table of contents. There were ten stories listed with page numbers. "Pick one."

Tyler pointed a shaking finger at the sixth story. Zack pointed at number three.

"No, no, not you," Beadlesberry said, poking Zack. "This is Tyler's story, you'll have your turn. Now where was I? Ah yes, interesting choice, The Wizard of Balalac." The old man turned the pages until he reached page six. There weren't any words on the pages. No wonder the book was so thin; there were only titles. He wondered where the stories were. Maybe this was just an index and there was another volume, like an encyclopedia.

"Nope, smart Tyler, this is it. The stories are there, you just have to know where to look for them." The old man's laugh sounded like bacon sizzling in a frying pan. "You look like you've seen a ghost, boy. Can't get one over on old Beadlesberry." Then he started coughing again from laughing so hard.

Tyler inched his chair away. The old man could read minds.

When the old man finally stopped coughing, Zack ventured to speak. "Are you okay? Do you need something, like water?"

Beadlesberry shook his head and patted Zack's arm. "You are a good boy, Zachary Vander. Got to watch the old lungs, you know. Cannot live without them." He laughed again. The boys sat up in alarm. The old man stopped, though, before the coughing could start up again. "Now where was I?" he said. "Oh yes, where are the stories? They are in there." He tapped a long thin finger at the page.

His curiosity won. Tyler forgot to keep perfectly still and silent. "What's in there? It's just a blank page. Is there invisible ink or something?"

Beadlesberry cackled again. "Ah, I see Thaddeus Trent did not tell you everything about this book, did he? Perhaps he thought you would not have come at all if you knew the truth."

Trent wanted to believe his uncle wouldn't get him into trouble. On the other hand, his uncle was always getting into trouble himself. This was looking worse every minute. He glanced toward the window, but the rain was still streaming down the glass. Then he jerked back around as another peal of thunder struck overhead. Zack was eyeing the door.

The old man was still speaking. "Let me explain. This book will take you on fabulous journeys to real and magical worlds. You choose the story and with the help of this magic pendant you become part of the story." The old man dangled a gold pendant attached to a black ribbon.

Tyler's mouth fell open. He shut it fast. It was just a magic trick, like the handkerchief. Tyler stared at the pendant. It was about three inches long and shaped like a flattened egg. There was a clear stone in the middle that sparkled in the flickering candlelight. Tyler could see most of the colors of the rainbow reflecting from the surface of the stone. Strange writing was carved into the gold.

"It's called a quartz crystal, supposed to come from the lost city of Atlantis. You can find out for yourself, daring Tyler, if you enter the story called City of the Sea. Crystals have magical properties."

Before he realized it, Tyler asked, "What is this writing?"

"Ah, he speaks," the old man said. "It is ancient Atlantian and means Guardian of the Traveler."

Tyler couldn't stop his voice. "How does it work?"

Beadlesberry grinned. "You hold the pendant in both hands. Then you choose a story and say the title aloud and say traverse. Before you know it you are in the story."

"In the story?" Tyler raised his eyebrows.

"Yes indeed, disbelieving Tyler. You don't just read a story from this book, you become part of the story." Beadlesberry peered at Tyler. "I see I have to explain further. The story you chose, Wizard of Balalac, takes place in the mythical land of Balara. The story would unfold with you as the main character. You would have to resolve the problem the Balarans are having in Balalac."

Zack was staring at the pendant. "What problem?" he asked.

"Can't tell you the whole story. Spoils the mystery." Beadlesberry said.

Tyler pursed his lips. "Okay, suppose I could go to this place Balalac in Balara. How would I get back here?”

“Excellent question, smart Tyler. You never left here. You are always in this bookstore, just inside the book and the book is on this table. Don’t stare at me as though I have lost my mind. Of course, the bookstore might not be there when you most need it.”

Tyler face turned white. “Wwwhat?” he stammered.

Beadlesberry shook his head. “Never mind. Pay no attention to what I just said. Not important. When you are ready to return, enter the bookstore, grasp the pendant and say bookshop reverse.”

“What bookshop are you talking about?” Zack asked.

“This bookshop, of course,” the old man said.

“You mean this bookshop is also in the story?” Tyler asked.

“Of course, of course. What did you think?

“But I thought you said I never left the bookstore,” Tyler said.

“Well, of course you have to leave it. How can you solve the problem and have a great adventure standing around in a dusty bookstore,” the old man said impatiently.

Tyler muttered, “I don’t think this is going to work.” Thunder resounded again, but further away. Tyler counted the seconds before the spark of lightening. The storm was moving away. He squeezed Zack's arm. Any minute now and they could escape.

Chapter 5

The Disappearance

Another thunderous peal blasted the silence and rain beat a tattoo on the windows. Beadlesberry slammed shut the book and the pendant disappeared. "Ah, Tyler. I thought you were daring like Thaddeus Trent. I believe I was mistaken."

"Wait." Tyler heard the word, but just couldn't believe his own ears. "Could we just try it for a few minutes?" It would never work anyway, so he had nothing to lose.

Beadlesberry beamed. "Of course, daring Tyler. Would five minutes be short enough?"

"Hey what about me?" Zack asked. "You're not going into some story and leave me here."

"Right, we both go together." Tyler said.

"Hmm. I've never sent two before. Well, I believe it will still work." Beadlesberry said grinning again.

Tyler asked. "You're sure we would come back here?"

"I have never lost anyone. Well, there was the young man who disappeared in Wales. Never mind, he wasn't careful. You on the other hand are very clever. You would never fight a fiery dragon."

The old man leaned closer. Tyler could smell his peppermint breath. "You are clever, are you not?" Tyler pressed back into the chair and nodded. The pendant reappeared, dangling from Beadlesberry's hand. The book flew open to page six. "Here, put the ribbon around your neck. Whatever you do, don't lose the pendant, or you won't ever be able to return." Beadlesberry cackled.

Tyler hesitated, then slipped the ribbon over his neck. He could feel the weight of the pendant pulling at the ribbon. There was a faint vibration against his chest. He grasped the pendant in both hands. It pulsed against his shaking fingers.

"Excellent, excellent," Beadlesberry said. "Now read the name of the story aloud and say traverse."

Tyler opened his mouth, but Beadlesberry shouted, "Wait, wait. Repeat what I told you about coming back."

Tyler frowned. "Um, hold the pendant in both hands and say bookshop reverse."

"NO!" shouted the old man. "You left out something."

Zack voice shook. "We have to be inside the bookstore."

Beadlesberry clapped his hands. "Yes, indeed. You are ready, valiant Tyler Trent and loyal friend Zachary Vander. Go forth and enter the world of Balara."

Tyler glanced at his watch. Five minutes. Not that he was really going anywhere. Tyler grasped the pendant.

Beadlesberry grinned. "Now where was I? Ah, yes, I wasn't anywhere. You were. Zachary, you should hold the pendant too, if you are going to go with Tyler."

Zack whispered, "If we disappear forever, my mother will kill you."

Tyler glared at Zack. "I'll disappear, too, remember?"

Hands shaking, the boys held the pendant in both hands and said, "The Wizard of Balalac, traverse."

Chapter 6

The Reappearance

Tyler closed his eyes against a flash of light. His body tingled and felt itchy. When he opened his eyes he was still standing in the bookstore. It was different.

Something was missing. The old man was gone. Tyler spun around and stared out of the window. It was no longer raining, but the light was dim.

"Where are we?" Tyler whispered.

"In the bookstore," Zack whispered.

"Why are we whispering?" Tyler asked.

Zack shrugged.

"Look around, Zack. Does anything look different?"

Zack turned. "Yeah, the old man is gone."

Tyler shook his head impatiently. "The sun is shining." He pulled Zack to the door. "I'm going outside. Are you ready?"

Tyler took a deep breath and opened the door. He and Zack stepped out into a sun-filled world of colorful little shops and houses. Soft green grass flowed in every direction, edged by colorful flower beds and small trees.

"This isn't New York," Zack said.

"No kidding. Where are the people?" Tyler said. "It's like those movies about nuclear bombs that wipe out everything."

"Do you think that's what happened here?" Zack asked, shrinking back toward the doorway. "Do you think there's radiativity. Maybe we should go back."

"There's no such word, Zack." Tyler shuddered. He sounded like is mother. "Anyway I don't think so. We wouldn't have been allowed to come here if there was danger of radioactivity."

"Radio…whatever, right," Zack said. "So what happened here?"

"How should I know," Tyler said, annoyed. "I just got here, too."

"Well, don't jump on me, Tyler, I'm scared."

"Yeah, well me too, Zack. "Maybe you're right, and we should go back."

The boys turned around. On the door of the bookshop was a sign We Close for Boiling Water.

Tyler and Zack looked at each other and said at the same time, "Boiling water?"

When they looked back all they saw was a plot of bright green grass.

"Where'd it go?" Zack shouted.

Tyler ran onto the grass, and spun around. "I don't know."

"What are we gonna do?" Zack yelled.

"How should I know?" Tyler hoped Uncle Tad got eaten by a shark. He would never speak to him again. "How could he do this to me?" Tyler wailed.

"Do what, who? What are you yelling about?" Zack screamed.

"I'm not yelling!" Tyler shouted. His voice softened. "Ok, I'm not yelling. We have to find Beadlesberry, right?" Zack nodded. "So let's move. Somebody has to be around." Tyler walked quickly down the street; Zack hurrying to catch up.

They walked faster and faster without seeing another person. The town abruptly ended and the road continued past fenced fields of blue vines and red-leaved plants. Around the next curve, they stopped short. "I don't believe it," Zack said, running into the field.

"Hey, come back, Zack." Tyler yelled. "It might not be safe." Tyler jumped back. He was staring into the eyes of a purple cow. The cow calmly lowered its head and pulled up a mouthful of grass.

Tyler back peddled until he was ten feet from the cow and looked around. Zack was standing on the grass by a pile of dried dung. There were more purple cows and some spotted, white and purple. This was impossible. Beadlesberry must have hypnotized him with the pendant and put this picture in his mind. There were no purple cows.

"Zack," he called softly so as not to scare the cows. Zack didn't answer. "Zack," he said louder.

"Do you see what I see?" Zack said pointing at the purple cow.

"Yeah, purple cows," Tyler said.

Zack started to move. "Watch it, Zack. You're standing next to cow dung."

Zack jumped and stepped back, rubbing the bottom of his shoes on the grass. “Yuck. So where are we?”

Tyler grinned, “I guess in a field of purple cows.”

Just then the cow moved toward them and mooed. The boys turned and ran back to the road. The cow stopped at the edge of the road and watched the boys walk quickly backwards away from it.

“I never heard of purple cows,” Zack said. “It’s like something a little kid would draw who never saw a cow. Gotta be hallucinating or something. Do you think Old Beadlesberry did something to us? Tyler, answer me. What…?”

“Shut up,” Tyler said.

“Hey, don’t tell me to shut up,” Zack said, angrily.

Tyler grabbed Zack’s arm. “No, listen, do you hear that?”

There was the rumble of wheels and the clip clop of hooves. A small, blue wagon rounded the curve pulled by a striped horse.

Zack tugged at Tyler's shirt. "Is that a zebra or a horse?"

"It looks like a striped horse." Tyler said.

“Oh, man this just gets weirderer by the minute,” Zack groaned.

The driver reined in the horse, or whatever it was, when he saw them. He was a small man with a long brown beard and wavy mustache. A wide straw hat covered his head. “Hello, strangers, visiting my lumpas?” He pointed toward the cows.

Lumpas? Trent never heard of lumpas. He glanced at Zack, who shrugged. Still thinking about purple lumpas, Trent stumbled over his words. “Uh, we just came to this place from the other side of, um, the country.” He couldn’t remember what Beadlesberry had called the country.

“Ah, must be from Balowag. Taller folks there,” the man said.

Balara, that was the name of the country. This must be Balalac. “Right, Balowag,” Tyler said.

“Tall people in Balowag,” Zack said.

The farmer nodded. “Off to Maidenspa? Don’t look sick. Not that it’s going to help anyway. Can’t use it anymore.” He thought that was very funny.

Tyler glanced at Zack and shrugged. “I thought this town was Maidenspa.”

“Yes, well, and no, too.” The man flicked the reins. “Get on. Give you a ride.”

Tyler frowned. “Well, where are we?”

"You are in Balalac."

"But isn't this the country of Balara?" Tyler asked.

"Yes, well, and no, too," the man repeated.

"I don't understand," Tyler said, wrinkling his brow in frustration.

"It's all the same. Not to worry. So do you want to go to Maidenspa or not?"

"Can the, um, horse pull us all?" Zack asked.

"Horse, huh? Is that what you folks call a pulla in Balowagian?" The farmer thought that was funnier than trying to explain Balara. He bent over double, his shoulders shaking. His hat fell off and he caught it and popped it back on his head. Finally, he looked up and nodded, his hat bobbing up and down. "Forgot foreign city folk don't know much about pullas."

The boys climbed on the wagon. It was so small they barely fit with their knees touching their chins. Tyler waited until they were moving. He looked at his watch. Thirty minutes had passed. How could that be?

Zack looked at the back of the farmer and said quietly to Tyler, "Where is he taking us? What if we can't find the bookstore again?"

"I don't know, Zack."

"We'll be here forever." Zack looked like he was going to cry.

"I thought you loved adventures."

Zack said, "Yeah, well this isn't the same as sneaking into a twenty-story hotel and riding outside elevators up and down for an hour."

"You're right. This is monstro weirdo. Maybe he's taking us to find the people. Then we can go back to town and look for the bookstore."

Zack sniffed. "This whole thing was just stupid."

Tyler muttered, "I hope there's a bookstore."

"Main Street, between the barber and the apothecary."

For a minute, Tyler thought the pulla had spoken, but it was the farmer. "I heard you talking back there on Main Street, where I picked you up. In fact you were standing right in front of it, or where it will be when it comes back. You're not the first visitor from back there, you know. Visitors always need the bookstore. Popular place, Old Beadlesberry's."

Tyler's mouth fell open. He looked at Zack. "Beadlesberry?" he mouthed. Tyler felt like he'd just fallen through the rabbit hole in Alice in Wonderland. All they needed was the Mad Hatter to throw a tea party.

Around the next curve the road split left and right. There was a sign in the middle of the fork pointing left to Balalac and right to Maidenspa. The farmer pulled on the left rein and the horse turned down the right fork.

"Did you see what he did? I feel like I'm a character in some book," Tyler whispered to Zack.

Zack looked at him like he was nuts. "You are in a book, stupid."

Then Tyler realized what he had said and felt like he had just slid another ten feetdown the rabbit hole. "I'm not stupid, I just forgot. I haven't seen any cars or trucks, have you? And where are all the people?"

"Beats me," Zack said. "Excuse me, sir, where is everybody?"

"Down to the spa," the farmer answered.

Tyler wrinkled his forehead. What spa? Maidenspa?

"What does boiling water mean?" Zack whispered.

"Maybe they take a coffee break," Tyler said.

"The whole town at the same time?" Zack said.

"How am I supposed to know? Do I look like a magician?" Tyler growled.

Zack put up his hands. "Hey don't get mad at me. I'm stuck here too, remember?"

Tyler sighed. "Sorry. It's just that it's already an hour and we were only supposed to be here for five minutes."

"Maybe time is different here," Zack offered. "You know, I was thinking we should go find this Maidenspa. Maybe that's where the boiling water is."

"And all the people," Tyler added.

"I hope Beadlesberry is there, where ever there is," Tyler said.

Chapter 7

The Legend of Maidenspa

After a few minutes, Tyler grabbed Zack. "Do you hear that?"

"What?" Zack shouted.

"Shsh. Listen. I hear voices, lots of voices," Tyler whispered.

"Okay, I hear them now. We must be close to Maidenspa," Zack said softly.

They rounded the next curve, and the cart rolled to a stop. The man climbed down. "Here you are, boys."

Where was here? Tyler and Zack jumped off the wagon. The voices were louder, coming from a large group of very short people gathered around billowing clouds of steam. They crept closer hoping no one would notice them, which Tyler knew was impossible, since he was so much taller than everybody else. Now they could see the outline of a lake, but the water was bubbling and smoking. "Boiling water," Tyler whispered.

A woman turned to them and said, "No baths today. You'll be cooked." She was round as an apple. Her hair hung down her back in a thick braid, tied with a ribbon.

Tyler figured he wouldn't learn anything if he didn't ask anything "Why is the water boiling?"

"A very good question. Right, Dismar?" she said.

The man standing next to her turned. "Indeed, indeed, Esmara. Excellent question and one not answered all these weeks."

"Alas, poor Dunby. So tragic," Esmara said sadly.

Tyler asked, "Why, what happened to Dunby?"

"Oh, nothing," Dismar answered.

Tyler could feel himself slide another foot down the rabbit hole. "Then why is it tragic?"

"Poor Dunby is the keeper of the spa."

"We come from uh…." Tyler looked at Zack.

"Um, Balowag," Zack finished.

Tyler nodded. "Right, we're Balowagans." Tyler could feel the laughter locked in his chest trying to break out. He could see Zack's hand covering his mouth.

Esmara smiled. "Of course, folks are taller in Balawag. Welcome to Maidenspa."

Dismar said, "I guess Balowagans don't know about the boiling waters."

Zack could speak now. "Uh, yeah. In fact

we don't even know anything about Maidenspa."

Dismar patted Zack on the back. "In that case. A long, long time ago a young girl never able to walk…."

"Born that way." Esmara interrupted.

Dismar continued the story. "Yes, well anyway, she couldn't walk and slid into the lake with her rolling chair. Pulled out by Dunby the First and from then on she could walk."

"That's so amazing," Tyler said.

"Yes, magical healing waters. Came from all over, people did, to bathe in the lake and be cured of all illnesses. Dunby became keeper of the spa." Dismar pointed to a life size statue of a man holding a girl in his arms set on a wooden platform overlooking the lake.

Esmara interrupted again. "Dunby's great, great, great grandson, well no one really knows how many greats, Dunby five, or is it six…? She rubbed the side of her head.

Dismar frowned at his wife. "That is not important. Dunby, whatever number, is the keeper of the spa today."

"Poor man. He has no sons to follow, just a daughter," Esmara said sadly.

Zack asked, "Can't a woman be the keeper?"

"Never happened yet, who knows?" Dismar said.

Tyler said, "So why is the water boiling?"

Esmara shrugged. "About a month ago everything in the town started shaking at the stroke of midnight and the next morning the water was boiling. It has happened every night since then. It is a terrible tragedy. Travelers come to be cured and go home still sick."

"Indeed," Dismar continued. "There is an old legend about a wizard and a dragon and two young warriors who will uncloak the wizard, slay the dragon and restore the waters." Dismar tilted his head and smiled at them. A glint of something malevolent flickered across his dark eyes, then was gone. Tyler's skin prickled. It happened so fast, maybe he had imagined it. He looked at Zack, frowning, but Zack was watching the steamy lake. Then Dismar shrugged and his eyes twinkled. "It is just a story. Who among us can really know?"

"Look, Dismar, the mayor." Esmara pointed toward the wooden stand.

Zack grabbed Tyler's arm. "I don't believe it. It's Beadlesberry."

The bony old man was dressed in his black suit, long gray hair sticking out around his head. The boys listened as Beadlesberry assured the people that everything was being done to find out why the earth shook and the water boiled. He said they were even sending for Gruen, the dragon hunter, just in case there was an angry dragon breathing fire on the lake.

The rock band banged away in Tyler's chest. He turned to Zack. "Did he say dragon?" Zack wagged his head up and down.

A large, red-faced man waved his hand and shouted. "Waste of time. No dragon tracks around the lake."

Esmara leaned close to Tyler. "My husband's cousin, Calamar, the confectioner. Always ready to argue, even as a child."

Confectioner? Tyler wished he had his mother or a dictionary. His mother was the better choice, then he wouldn't be here watching a boiling lake and listening to talk of dragon hunters.

Esmara was still speaking. "Ask for chocolate marshmallow squares, he argues coconut butterscotch rounds." Aha, Tyler thought, the candy man.

Beadlesberry finished his speech with a promise that everything was being done that could be done. People turned to leave. Tyler and Zack pushed their way through the crowd to get to Beadlesberry, but he was gone by the time they got to the stand.

"Where do you think you are going?" A deep voice said from behind them.

The boys turned facing a man almost as thin as Beadlesberry. He had long light hair that came to his shoulders and dead black eyes. There was a girl beside him covering her face with her hands. From what they could see of her hair, she might have been his daughter. "We're looking for the Mayor," Zack said quickly.

"You were pushing. We do not like those who push in Balalac. Be very careful, young warriors," he said grimly, walking away with the girl.

Tyler wondered why he had called them young warriors. "I'm sorry, sir," he called. The man looked back once, his dead eyes drilling holes in

Tyler's head. He shivered. "Man, a real weirdo. So where'd Beadlesberry go?" Tyler said, peering over the crowd. He noticed a large black bird sitting on the branch of a crooked tree staring at him, but no Beadlesberry. Weird times ten.

Zack shrugged, "Must have done his famous disappearing act. Let's go back into town and find the bookstore and go home."

Tyler was about to open his mouth to suggest that the bookstore might still be invisible, when he heard muffled sobbing. Tyler bent down and peered under the wooden stand. A girl about their age was huddled in the grass. All he could see was long black hair covering her shaking shoulders. Tyler pulled Zack down on the grass and asked, "You okay?"

She sat up startled and bumped her head on the wooden slats of the stand. She rubbed her head and turned her tear-streaked face toward him. Tyler tingled. She was so tiny and beautiful. "I'm sorry," he said. "I didn't mean to scare you. I heard you crying."

She looked at them with bright, wet eyes. A single tear spilled over her eyelid and slid down her cheek. "I wasn't crying, thank you. There was a piece of dirt in my eye."

"Okay, fine. My name's Tyler Trent and this is Zack Vander. We're, um, from Balowag."

"Hi," Zack said.

The girl crawled out from under the stand and stood there, hands on hips "Ellaby."

"Wait," Zack said. "Let me guess. Dunby, Ellaby. I bet you're the spa keeper's daughter."

Ellaby nodded, wiping her eyes with the back of her hand. Trent looked at his friend in astonishment. Zack grinned. "It's easy, you know, word endings."

It was one of those moments Tyler's mother always referred to as an "aha" or his father as a revelation. "Um, er ….are you sure you're all right, Ellaby?" Tyler asked, kicking himself for babbling.

Ellaby stuck her chin in the air. "I am just fine, thank you."

Zack said, "This must be hard for you, I mean with the lake boiling and all that."

Ellaby looked toward the statue of Dunby the First. "It is Papa who worries all the time; who cannot sleep or eat. People would come for the water, buy things in Balalac and stay at the Inn. No more travelers. No more curing sick people," she said swiping at another tear that threatened to fall off the end of her nose.

"Ellaby, Ellaby." A man's voice called.

Ellaby jumped, sniffing. "Papa. Come along, but please do not tell him I said anything, it would only upset him." She took each of their hands and led them across the field toward a gigantic house. There were three levels, ten peaks in the roof and dozens of windows. Tyler counted 4 chimneys and that was just the front. A deep purple porch wrapped around like a belt. There was a sign, THE MAIDENSPA INN, perched on the top of a pole along the side of the porch. Tyler wished he had taken a camera. Who would ever believe this amazing house? A small, spotted, yellow dog jumped off the porch and streaked across the grass, yapping and jumping at their legs. Zack reached down to pet it, but the dog growled.

"Hush, Pottaby, silly boy," Ellaby said sternly. "Friends." The dog sniffed their feet and then their extended hands. He seemed to approve and allowed Zack to rub his head. The dog pranced around their feet as they followed Ellaby to the house. A black-haired man stood on the porch. His shoulders drooped and his striped shirt hung loosely on his thin body, covering baggy pants. He had the same eyes as Ellaby, dulled with sadness. "Papa, meet Tyler Trent and his friend Zack Vander. They have come all the way from Balowag."

Dunby reached out and grasped their hands in both of his. "Welcome to Maidenpa. It is so regretful, that I cannot offer you the waters of the lake, although you both look healthy enough. You are welcome to spend time here. Perhaps we will soon solve the problem of the boiling water."

"I'm sorry about Maidenspa, sir," Tylersaid.

"Me too," Zack said. "Do you really think it could be a dragon?"

Dunby shrugged. "One never can know. Things do appear suspiciously dragonlike. Perhaps Gruen, the mighty, can determine the truth. But please, enough of this discussion. Come inside, dinner is ready."

Tylershook his head. "Oh, we can't stay. We have to go back into town."

"But darkness comes soon," Ellaby said, pointing at the setting sun. "You cannot walk to town after dark. It is not safe anymore."

"Ellaby speaks truth. Stay here tonight and go to town tomorrow morning," Dunby said, opening the door.

"Oh man, my mom's gonna kill me," Zack muttered.

"We really have to go home tonight," Tylersaid.

"Impossible," Dunby said. "Impossible to go to Balalac at night, how would you go all the way to Balowag?"

"It is not safe to go so far in the dark," Ellaby said.

Dunby leaned closer. "What if there is a dragon?"

Fingers of fear crept down Tyler's spine. He could see it so clearly. He and Zack are walking in the moonlight down the deserted road. All around them strange noises come from the deep, dark forests. Suddenly they hear the crashing of giant feet and a twenty-foot green scaly beast is suddenly bearing down on them, roaring and spitting fire. His tail whips around taking down trees like they were twigs. Tylershivered. "We need to talk a minute." He pulled Zack down the steps and away from the porch. "Listen, maybe it's not such a good idea to go back into town tonight. The bookstore may not even be there."

Zack made a face. "You know how I hate it when you're right. Even if it's there, it'll probably be closed. We'll never find Beadlesberry tonight."

Tyler relaxed. "Do you think time is different here? Maybe it's just a few minutes back in our world and not a whole day."

"I sure hope so or there's gonna be a manhunt for us by tomorrow. My dad knows everybody, even the mayor." Zack added. Zack's father was a lawyer.

"I sure wish we hadn't done this. I never expected it to work. Leave it to my Uncle Tad to get me in hot water," Tyler said.

Zack laughed and Tyler frowned, "What's so funny."

"Hot water?"

"Oh man, very funny, very funny." Tyler turned his back before Zack could see the big grin on his face. Zack punched his shoulder and laughed harder.

Pottaby ran around in circles. Zack reached down and scratched his ears. The little spotted dog rolled over on his back, four legs sticking straight up in the air. Zack bent down and tickled his stomach. Then he looked up at Tyler. "My mom's gonna be pissed off when I'm not there for dinner tonight."

Tyler said, "They'll probably think we're at each other's apartment."

"Just so long as they don't get together and compare notes, at least not until tomorrow. Oh man, what a mess!" Zack shook his head.

"Listen, Zack, I'm real sorry I got you into this. It's all my fault," Tyler moaned.

Zack jumped up. "Hey, I went along, you didn't break my arm. Besides, if anyone's to blame it's your Uncle Tad. And you know what, this might be fun. Anyway, I think Ellaby likes you."

Tyler punched Zack in the arm. "Jerk."

Zack socked him back. "Dork."

The boys climbed the steps to the gold porch, Pottaby yapping beside them. Ellaby smiled and took Tyler's hand. His face burned bright red, and he could feel Zack laughing beside him. He poked Zack in the ribs, hard. Zack just laughed harder. Tyler wriggled his hand out of Ellaby's. "So what's for dinner?"

"Boiled fish," Ellaby answered.

Tyler's stomach jumped. He pointed back to the steaming lake. "You mean…?"

Ellaby laughed. "Oh, no, silly, not from the lake. "Tonight we are serving squank squillamara from the fishery."

"Uh huh," Tyler said, his stomach leaping higher.

"Just watch the bones," Ellaby said. "Oh, and please tell Crumble that you liked it."

Tyler stopped in his tracks. "Crumble?"

Ellaby turned in the doorway. "Yes, Crumble. She is our housekeeper and an excellent cook. Her husband, Bramble, is the caretaker and gardener. They have been here since before Papa was born."

Tyler could hear Zack sniggering behind him. He swung his arm back and connected with Zack's body. "Ouch. What'd you do that for?" Zack complained.

Tyler smiled at Ellaby. "We just love squank squillimara," he said, following Ellaby into the Inn.

Chapter 8

The Stairway to Nowhere

Tyler stared at the scaly red fish staring up at him from the plate. It lay limp on the plate, surrounded by long stems that looked like a cross between green beans and celery stalks. He looked up at the roly poly woman standing in the doorway, tapping a wooden spoon against her side. Tyler grinned and picked up his fork. "Looks great, Crumble." Then he suddenly remembered his father's comment one night in a fancy French restaurant. "Very nice presentation."

Crumble grinned. "I just knew you boys would be hungry after your long journey from Balowag. Well, eat up. There is popps for dessert." Great, Tyler thought, ice cream.

Tyler nodded, prodding the fish. "How do you eat this?" He pushed his fork under the scales and pulled out a piece of white flesh. It looked like lobster meat. Tyler shut his eyes and put the forkful in his mouth. "Hey, it even tastes like lobster."

Zack stared at the red fish. "Are you sure? I don't like lobster much."

Tyler shoved more fish in his mouth.

"Would I lie to you, Zack," he mumbled through the food. Out of the corner of his eye, Tyler watched Zack pick out a piece of white meat from under the scales and touch it to his lips. "Try opening your mouth. It helps."

"Just shut up, okay? I'm working on it," Zack said. Then he took a deep breath and pushed the fork between his teeth. He chewed slowly. "Tastes more like chicken to me."

"Lobster," Tyler said.

"Chicken, it tastes like chicken," Zack insisted.

Tyler shrugged. "Whatever." Soon, there was nothing left on their plates but the skeleton of a fish. "I can't believe I even ate those vegetable things," Tyler said. "I never eat vegetable things. They reminded me of corn on the cob."

"Mashed potatoes," Zack said.

"So, you boys enjoyed dinner?" The boys jumped. Crumble was standing behind them holding a large silver tray.

"Delicious, thank you," Zack said quickly.

"Right," Tyler added. "Wonderful."

Crumble beamed. "Good. It has been too long since guests have come to the Inn. Now, you get popps for dessert." She placed two small bowls filled with pink balls in front of them and gathered up the dirty plates.

Tyler waited until she had left and said, "I thought popps were ice cream. This looks suspiciously like melon balls." He licked a spoonful of the popps. "It is melon, canteloupe."

Zack licked his spoon. "More like watermelon. You know this is really weird. We each think the food tastes like something we really like."

Tyler said, "This must be part of the mythical, magical, mystery story side of the book."

Zack shook his head. "You know you spend too much time with your mother, the English teacher."

Tyler laughed. "I bet she'd love to hear you say that."

"Say what?" Ellaby said from the doorway.

"Oh, just that the meal was delicious," Zack said quickly.

"Oh, yeah, especially the popps," Tyler added.

"That is good. Come along, I'll show you to your rooms." Ellaby said. "I don't suppose you brought any clothes with you." Tyler and Zack shook their heads. "That is all right. There are extra clothes in your room. People forget and leave them behind. Visitors to Maidenspa seem to be very absentminded, and they are always losing something."

"Like the bookshop," Zack muttered as they followed her into the great hall. Three staircases rose in different directions from a central landing, winding around in dizzying circles. Ellaby reached the landing and stepped onto the staircase winding to the right. Tyler tried to follow the three staircases up with his eye, but they seemed to turn off in too many directions at once. Now he was thoroughly confused. He rubbed his hand along the dark wooden railing. A soft blue carpet fastened to each step deadened the sound of his feet.

They climbed up in a tight circle until they reached a landing with a long window of colored glass. Tyler peered out and saw the lake. The water was still now, with only an occasional bubble popping here and there. A fine vapor of steam hovered over the water.

Tyler turned and followed Ellaby and Zack down a narrow hallway. Ellaby opened one door and then another across the hall. "I think you will be comfortable here. The bathroom is next door. I have put fresh towels in there for you. If you need anything tonight, just ring this bell." She pointed to a large iron bell hanging on the wall and pulled the chain.

Zack covered his ears at the loud bonging sound. "I bet you can hear that out at the lake," he said.

Ellaby giggled. Tyler immediately thought of his mother's wind chimes tinkling on the balcony. "So where do the other staircases lead?"

"Just to other parts of the Inn. Papa and I live up the middle staircase. Crumble and Bramble live downstairs behind the kitchen," Ellaby explained.

"I've never been in a house with three staircases," Zack said.

"Oh there are more than three," Ellaby said. "You just cannot see them."

"Where are they?" Zack asked.

"Behind walls."

Zack looked bewildered. "What good are staircases if they're behind walls? Like, where do they go?"

"Oh, they don't go anywhere, Zack. Just like the doors that open to nothing," Ellaby answered.

"Come on," he said. "How can doors go nowhere?"

Ellaby took his hand and pulled him down the hall to the last door. "Open it."

Tyler stood behind her watching as Zack rubbed his hands together and turned the doorknob. The door creaked open. There was nothing but blackness. Zack reached in and felt around. "There's nothing there," he said, stepping back.

Tyler reached around him and pushed his arm through the doorway. He couldn't feel anything. He waved his arm in a wide circle. There was still nothing there. He turned to Ellaby. "What would happen if I stepped through the doorway?"

"I don't know. No one has ever tried to enter one of the doorways to nothing."

Zack said, "You mean there's more than one of these?"

"Oh yes," Ellaby said. "There are many doorways to nothing in the

Inn."

"Where are the other staircases?" Tyler asked.

"They don't go anywhere either," Ellaby said. "I told you that."

"I know, I know. I just wondered where they are so I don't take one by accident," Tyler said.

"Tyler and Zack, I think you are playing fun with me. You cannot possibly use a staircase you cannot find, that would take you nowhere if you did find it."

Tyler tilted his head and looked at Zack, who smirked. "Good night, Ellaby."

"Good night Tyler, good night Zack. Sleep well until midnight." She marched off down the corridor.

"What did she mean, until midnight?" Tyler asked.

"How should I know?" Zack answered. "Never mind that. You feel up to finding a hidden staircase to nowhere?"

Tyler turned back to the door to nothing. "I'd rather find out what's on the other side of this door." He turned the handle and pulled, but the door didn't budge. He pulled harder, but the door refused to move. "Come on, give me a hand."

Zack put his hands over Tyler's and pulled with him. The door remained shut. "I don't believe it," Tyler said. "It was just open."

"More magic?" Zack said. "Maybe Ellaby's a witch."

"Yeah, sure, the Wizard of Maidenspa's an eleven year old girl." Tyler laughed nervously. Then he wondered why a wizard couldn't be a girl. What did you call a female wizard anyway, a wizardess? This was stupid; she wouldn't put a spell on the lake and ruin her own father. "That's it, I'm going to bed. You can find your own hidden staircase."

Just then he heard the patter of nails against the floor and Pottaby emerged from the shadows. He sat down and panted at them. Tyler bent down and lifted the dog in his arms. He scratched a dot under Pottaby's left ear and went back down the hall to his room. He put the dog, if that was what they were called here, on the bed and looked around. The walls were painted in red stripes. The bed was large and had four pillars in each corner that rose to the high ceiling. The bed cover was overlapping circles of every imaginable shade of orange.

A low wooden chest sat on the floor at the foot of the bed. There was a rocking chair in one corner and a long table between the bed and the rocker. A lamp that looked like a barrel sat on the table next to a bowl filled with strange pink balls. Tyler picked up a ball and sniffed. It smelled like melon. He licked it and then took a bite. It looked like an apple but tasted like cantaloupe. He ate the whole thing and looked around for the trash can. Tyler shrugged and put the core on the table next to the bowl. He would get rid of it tomorrow.

"Tyler, help."

Pottaby leaped off the bed and pattered out into the hall. Tyler followed him. "Zack, where are you?" he called.

Zack's voice sounded far away. "I'm in the wall."

"What are you talking about? Stop playing games," Tyler said angrily.

"I'm not playing games. I'm in the wall. I opened a door and there was this staircase. Now I can't find my way back." Zack's voice was growing fainter.

"Don't move. You're getting further away. Just stand still." Tyler yelled. "Tell me which door you went in."

"I don't know. Just get me out of here. Ring the bell or something."

Tyler wasn't about to call Ellaby or Dunby to search for Zack. They would think he was an idiot who couldn't find his own friend, even if he was somewhere in the walls. Besides, what if they got mad and threw them out. He thought about a dragon lurking in the woods. Get real, Tyler. Pottaby barked. Tyler turned toward the sound but couldn't see anything down the dark corridor. He followed the sound of the dog and found him sitting in front of a narrow door, wagging his tail.

"Is he in there?" Tyler asked the dog. Like he was really gonna answer. But Pottaby did answer. He stood up against the door and barked. "Okay, good dog." Tyler grasped the doorknob and prayed it would turn. Yes, the door swung open and there was a narrow staircase that went down into blackness. "Zack, are you there?" he called.

"I'm somewhere, Tyler, I just don't know where." Zack yelled.

Tyler rolled his eyes. "Listen, I'm at the top of a narrow staircase. I'm going to find some rope or something to leave a trail back up and then I'm coming down to find you. Hang in."

"Hurry up, Tyler. I need to pee."

Great, Tyler thought. He ran back to the room and looked around for string or rope. He opened the chest but there were only clothes. Nothing. Then he had an idea. He pulled the bedspread off and then the sheets. He twisted them and tied them together.

Racing back to the door, he tied one end around the doorknob and holding the sheet he started down the staircase unwinding it as he descended. "I hope I don't run out of sheets before I get to Zack," he mumbled.

Pottaby sat quietly by the open door. It grew darker as he climbed away from the faint light of the hallway. The staircase suddenly turned sharply to the left. "Gotta remember this. Turn right going back up," he said to himself. He was almost out of his makeshift safety rope, when the stairway turned right. "Okay, left, then right." Tyler stopped and called, "Zack, can you hear me."

"Great, you found me," Zack shouted in his ear.

Tyler nearly fell backwards down the stairs. He grabbed the front of Zack's shirt to keep from falling. "Of all the stupid, crazy things to do," he screamed. "You nuts?"

"Calm down, Tyler. You sound like my mother when I locked Carrie in my uncle's tool shed last week."

"You what?" Tyler yelled.

"Nothing happened to her. Like Jupiter, Saturn and Mars were all lined up in the sky and I was concentrating on finding them with my

binoculars. She wouldn't shut up about this stupid something or other she was trying to do and she wouldn't go away. So…"

"…You locked her in the shed." Tyler finished "Brilliant move."

"Okay, it wasn't so smart. As soon as I let her out she ran right to my Mom and told on me."

"Well, what did you expect her to do?" Tyler asked as he started back up the stairs.

Zack held onto Tyler's belt and crept along behind him. "Just what she did, I guess."

"Okay," Tyler said. "Case closed. Now shut up and stay right behind me." Tyler muttered, "Left, then right, left, then right, left, then right." He rolled up the sheet as he followed it up the steps. The staircase angled off to the left and he turned with it. A few more feet and it turned right. Now he could see a faint light from the door. The sheet shone white against the dark staircase.

Pottaby started barking again. Then the little dog took the sheet in his mouth and started to pull on it. "Stop, Pottaby. I can't move that fast, it's too dark," Tyler called, but the dog kept pulling. Tyler moved faster. "Hurry up, Zack, something's wrong. Pottaby's all excited."

The boys climbed the stairs faster and faster and piled out of the door with Pottaby yapping at their heels. Tyler snatched the sheet from the doorknob just as the door slammed shut and disappeared.

Zack stared at the blank wall. "Did you just see what I saw?"

Tyler was too shocked to do anything but nod.

Zack ran his hands over the wall. "It's gone. It just disappeared. I would have disappeared with it. Oh my God. I would have disappeared into the wall forever." Zack backed up in a panic. "I would have died in there." He grabbed Tyler by the shoulders. "You saved my life, you saved my life. Oh my God."

Tyler shook Zack. "Stop it. You wouldn't have died. There's probably another door someplace else. Besides if Pottaby hadn't warned us I would have been in there with you."

"Right, and we would have died together. Beadlesberry never said we could die. He lied to us. I want to go home," Zack wailed.

Tyler remembered that the old man had talked about some kid that was probably eaten by a dragon in Wales or Scotland. The hallway suddenly felt cold. Tyler shivered. He couldn't stop thinking about being walled up in the dark staircase. He would never say it to Zack or anyone, but he really wanted his mother. He wanted her to tuck him into bed like he was a little boy. He wanted the smell of fresh chocolate chip cookies. He even wanted her to correct his English. He would do his homework every night and read five books a week. He just wanted to go home. What he said instead was, "I'm going to bed."

Zack took Pottaby into his room. He stuck his head around the doorway. "Hey, Tyler, would you mind leaving your door open and I'll leave mine open too. You know, just in case."

Tyler was only too happy to agree. He threw the sheets back on the bed not even bothering to tuck them in. Let Crumble think he was a restless sleeper. Tyler took off his shoes and crawled under the covers, clothes and all. He pulled out the pendant and wrapped his hand around it. Please God, please let the bookstore be there tomorrow. He looked at his watch that glowed in the dark and closed his eyes. It was eleven o'clock.

Chapter 9

Earthquake

The shaking was barely detectable when it first began. Tyler eyes flew open. The room was black, except for a sliver of silver moonlight creeping under the curtains and across the blanket. Then the bed seemed to move a few inches across the room. Tyler gripped the edges of the mattress and stared into the blackness. The shaking started again, stronger this time.

Tyler rolled across the bed. He wished he'd paid more attention in Earth science. Were you supposed to run outside or hide in the tub? Maybe that was for tornadoes. You couldn't run outside in a tornado, you'd get sucked away. Did you run outside in an earthquake? Maybe not in New York, where tall buildings could fall on you. He thought about sliding under the bed. What if the roof caved in and landed on the bed and crushed him. Do something, his brain screamed, before you get dead.

Tyler leaped out of bed and ran into the hall. He crashed into Zack. "What's going on?" he screamed.

"How should I know?" Zack yelled, pulling him down the stairs.

Tyler could hear Pottaby barking. Dunby ran out of the dining room. "In here, boys, it is best to be beside the table."

Ellaby was sitting next to the huge dining room table holding a wriggling Pottaby. Tyler and Zack collapsed beside her. "What's happening?" Zack asked.

Ellaby sighed. "It is the same thing every night at the stroke of twelve."

"I never heard of an earthquake happening every night at exactly the same time." Tyler said.

Dunby sat beside them. "We don't really believe it is an earthquake.

"So what is it?" Tyler asked.

Ellaby looked at her father. "We think it may be a dragon," she whispered.

Tyler almost laughed, but he saw how serious they were. He took a deep breath for control and said, "Okay, why?"

"That's what we don't know," Dunby said. "Beadlesberry thinks it is connected to the boiling spa."

Zack said, "What does one thing have to do with the other?"

Ellaby said, "The earth shakes every night and the spa is always boiling in the morning."

"So a dragon is breathing fire on the water and making it boil and the earth shakes when it walks back and forth?" Tyler asked.

Ellaby and Dunby both nodded.

"Why?" both boys said at the same time.

Ellaby and Dunby looked at each other and shrugged.

"You must have some idea?" Zack asked.

Ellaby hugged Pottaby closer and whispered so faintly that the boys had to lean over to hear. "A wizard."

"A wizard?" they said at the same time.

"Hush," Ellaby whispered louder. "He might hear you."

"Who might hear me?" Tyler asked.

"The wizard," she said.

Tyler wondered if these people weren't just a little bit crazy. First it was dragons and now wizards. Maybe he should go along with the idea and humor them. He nodded like he knew all about wizards. Then he turned to Zack and winked. "So tell me about this wizard. Who is he and why is he doing this?"

Dunby spoke. "It is just a tale that has been told since the first Dunby was Keeper of the Spa. One day a wizard would appear at Maidenspa and cast a spell causing the earth to shake and the water to boil."

Ellaby continued. "The story also tells of two young warriors who would expose the wizard and save Maidenspa." She looked up at Tyler, her eyes shining in the moonlight.

Zack giggled nervously. "Uh, oh, trouble."

Tyler rammed him with an elbow and Zack grunted. "So, who's the wizard?" Tyler asked.

"It is only a folk story," Dunby said quietly.

No one spoke. The night had grown very still. Speckles of moonlight peeked through windows. The floor had stopped shaking and an owl hooted outside. Somewhere, an animal screamed.

Dunby stood up and announced that it was now safe to go back to bed. They all trooped upstairs in silence. When he finally fell asleep after what seemed like hours, but was really only minutes, Tyler dreamed that a giant green monster was stomping through the streets of New York, crushing cars and buildings in its wake. Only the tall buildings were all pink, blue, and yellow.

Tyler blinked at the sunlight streaming in the window. He stretched and yawned. A jackhammer jarred his brain. They must be tearing up the street again, he thought. Then Tyler sat up. This wasn't New York. This was Maidenspa or Balalac, or whatever. There were no streets and no jackhammers. He ran to the window. A small brown bird with a red head beat a tattoo against the tree outside. Tyler pressed his nose against the glass. City kids never got to see woodpeckers, just pigeons and starlings, or maybe sparrows. How could such a small bird make such a racket?

"Hey, what are you doing?"

Tyler spun around. "You scared me, man. Don't sneak up like that."

Zack smirked. "Sorry. What's so interesting out there? Ellaby, maybe?"

"Shut up about her, okay? Just come over here and look at the tree."

Zack looked out the window. "It's a tree."

Tyler peered over his shoulder, but the bird was gone. "There was a woodpecker. It sounded like a jackhammer. For a minute I thought I was back home in my own bed."

"No such luck," Zack said. "Can you believe what happened last night?"

"Do you mean the invisible door to the stairway to nowhere or the midnight earthquake caused by an angry dragon?" Tyler asked.

"Pick one," Zack suggested. Then Tyler told him about his dream. "Sounds like Godzilla takes Tokyo," Zack said.

"More like, Dragon takes Maidenspa," Tyler said.

"Get dressed, Tyler. We'd better get moving and find Beadlesberry."

"I hope breakfast is better than last night's dinner. Did you see that fish? It had four eyes," Tyler said, shuddering.

"What about the tentacles on the end of the fins. Barf!" Zack stuck his finger in his mouth and gagged.

"I don't think I'll ever eat fish again. In fact, I might just become a vegetarian after this," Tyler mumbled as he pulled his tee shirt over his head.

"Do you think they serve pancakes in this place?" Zack asked. "I'm afraid to think about the eggs."

"Probably black," Tyler added, zipping his jeans.

Zack beat his hands in rhythm against the wall. "Black eggs and ham, black eggs and ham."

Tyler grabbed his jacket. "Come on, whatever they have, we can at least eat some bread and butter."

"The butter probably looks like dried blood clots," Zack snorted, following Tyler down the stairs.

"Good morning, Tyler, Zack," Ellaby said at the foot of the staircase. Two black braids hung down her back, tied with large ribbons.

Zack leaned forward and whispered, "She likes you."

Tyler shoved his elbow in Zack's ribs. "Morning, Ellaby. Nice day."

Zack peered over his shoulder. "Morning, Ellaby."

"Would you boys like some breakfast? Crumble made pancakes."

"Love some," Zack said, pushing past Tyler and racing down the stairs.

The walls of the dining room were papered in huge multi-colored flowers that seemed to jump out in the morning sunlight. It was like being in the middle of a jungle. The boys sat at the long table that could seat twenty easily, but only had two places set. There was a glass of blue-green juice at each place. Tyler picked up the glass and sniffed. It smelled like fruit, but he couldn't place what kind. He didn't know anybody who drank blue-green juice. He put it down as Ellaby came in with a platter of pancakes.

Zack grinned. "I told you," he whispered, reaching over with his fork to spear three pancakes.

"There is prickleberry syrup over there and milk in that pitcher," Ellaby said, pointing to the center of the table. Tyler hoped the purple color of the pitcher was the glass and not the milk inside.

Zack muttered, "Figures, purple milk."

"What kind of juice is this, Ellaby?" Tyler asked, ignoring Zack.

"Now you are just being silly, Tyler. Surely you have flyfruit in Balowag." With that, she marched back into the kitchen.

Zack laughed. "Sure, Tyler, haven't you ever had flyfruit juice. Must be where the fruit fly comes from."

"Shut up," Tyler said, staring balefully at the pancakes. He put one on his plate and poured some prickleberry syrup over it. Zack was shoveling huge chunks of pancakes into his mouth, dripping syrup down his chin. Tyler took a small piece and sniffed it. Then he put it in his mouth. Mmm, sweet and chewy. He took three more pancakes and liberally poured syrup over them. Then he began stuffing his mouth with forkfuls of food.

"This tastes like real pancakes with syrup," Zack said. Tyler just nodded, his mouth too full to answer. He thought they were more like waffles with whipped cream. At least they didn't have eyes and scales.

Ellaby stood in the doorway, wiping her hands on a towel. "I see you are enjoying the pancakes."

"Mmm," Tyler mumbled through a mouthful of food.

"Terrific," Zack said before plunging another fork of pancakes through his lips.

Tyler swallowed his last mouthful and looked balefully at the purple pitcher. Tyler poured half a glass and took a sip. It tasted like his mother's two percent milk. "Ellaby, is the milk always lavender purple?"

Ellaby stared at him. "Well, yes, lumpas are purple, so their milk is purple."

Lumpas, cows, Tyler thought. Purple cows, purple milk, sure. "Oh right, we have brown cows, uh lumpas, where we come from. They give brown milk. We call it chocolate milk."

Zack laughed so hard he started choking. Tyler smacked him on the back.

"Hey, that hurt," Zack said when he could breathe again.

"Is that so? I was trying to save your life. I thought you were choking on the milk," Tyler said wickedly.

"Very funny," Zack grumbled. Then he thought of chocolate milk coming from brown cows, and started laughing again. Tyler put his hand over his mouth to hide his grin.

Ellaby stared at the boys. "I just don't see what's so funny about our milk."

Zack took a deep breath. "Sorry, Ellaby. Where's Crumble? The pancakes were great."

"She's upstairs making the beds," Ellaby said. "I'll tell her you said so, Tyler."

The boys were suddenly serious. "I guess it's safe to walk to town now and find the bookstore," Tyler said, wiping his mouth.

Ellaby shrugged. "Oh, well, it might not be there."

Tyler stood up and started to clear his plate. "Yeah, well, it kind of disappeared yesterday."

"Like the door last night," Zack mumbled.

"It does that sometimes." Ellaby's eyes glinted. Tyler wondered if she had heard Zack. Did she know what they were doing last night? He picked up his plate, but Ellaby

took it from him. “Oh no, this is an inn. You are our guest. What do you need at the bookstore?”

Zack started to speak, but Tyler looked at him and shook his head. “We want to check out information on dragons and wizards. Right, Zack?”

Zack nodded. “Sure, wizards and dragons.”

Ellaby smiled. “I just knew you were the two young warriors who would save us.”

“Warriors, us? I don’t think so,” Tyler said. Ellaby just continued to smile as she walked back into the kitchen. Oh boy, Tyler thought, now we’re really in trouble. We're leaving Maidenspa just in time. He thought he just might miss Ellaby a little bit. Don't be a jerk, he said to himself; she's just a character in a story. He turned to Zack. "You coming?"

"Sure. I was just waiting for you to stop dreaming about Ellaby."

Tyler swiped at Zack, but he ducked and ran out the door. Tyler chased after him. Pottaby sat on the porch and watched the boys race down the road. Then he turned back into the house, his nails tapping softly on the floor.

Chapter 10

The Lost Pendant

The road to the town of Balalac circled the boiling lake. Steam rose in great clouds out of the bubbling water. Tyler and Zack walked quickly away toward town. Today there were people on the streets, going in and out of the shops. Everyone wore flowered clothing that mingled like a moving botanical garden. Zack pulled Tyler's sleeve and pointed down the street. "Look, isn't that the apothecary? Let's hope the bookstore is on the other side."

They ran toward the yellow sign showing a giant mortar and pestle. Sometimes he did pay attention in science. His teacher had once used a mortar and pestle to mix flour and water into a paste. Tyler wondered if Dismar still mixed his medicines in a stone bowl with a stone grinding tool. As they passed the apothecary, Tyler could see Dismar behind the counter. The image of Dismar's eyes flickering with evil for that second yesterday pushed him to move faster before Dismar could see him. He thought he saw a movement out of the corner of his eye, but it was gone in a flash. Tyler hoped it was just his own reflection in the window. He stopped short behind Zack. The bookstore was there.

Thank you God, he thought and reached into his shirt for the pendant. It was gone. Tyler patted his shirt and even pulled his jeans out to see if it had slipped under the waistband. "It's gone, Zack, it's gone."

Zack turned, bumping into Tyler. "What's gone?"

"The pendant, the pendant." Tyler's voice was shrill. "It's gone."

Zack grabbed Tyler's shoulders and shook him hard. "How can it be gone? You didn't take it off did you?"

"No. And stop shaking me," Tyler shouted. People had stopped and were looking at them. Zack opened the door to the bookshop and pulled Tyler inside.

"May I help you?"

The boys stood like statues for ten seconds and then whirled around shouting at the same time. "Where were you last night?"

"Why, right here of course. I live behind the shop," Beadlesberry said. "Do I know you?"

Tyler wanted to scream. "Of course you know us, you sent us here."

The old man seemed puzzled. "I do not believe I have ever seen you before in my life."

Now Tyler was sure he was going insane. Next thing he would see was a grinning Cheshire cat sitting on one of the bookshelves. This wasn't happening. He must still be in his own room on Friday night having a nightmare. Why couldn't he wake up?

"Mr. Beadlesberry, my name is Tyler Trent and this is my friend Zack Vander. We came here from your bookshop in New York City through the Book of Mysteries, using the pendant. But now I can't find the pendant and we have to go home."

"Right," Zack said very fast. "Last night we tried to find you but the bookstore disappeared and then we found the boiling lake and you were talking about dragon hunters and then we met Ellaby and stayed at the inn and the earth shook and…." Zack puffed trying to suck in more air.

Beadlesberry scratched his head. "New York City?"

"Oh my God," Zack started to walk in circles, smacking the side of his head with his fist. "I'm going nuts, I'm going nuts."

"Young man, perhaps you should sit down. I shall get you some flyfruit punch. Yes indeed, just the thing," the old man said, pushing books off a chair.

"I don't want to sit down. I don't want buggy juice. I want to go home," Zack wailed.

"Of course, of course," Beadlesberry said soothingly. "Perhaps I should call Dismar, the apothecary, to give you something to calm you." He turned to the door.

Tyler shouted, "No, wait. Zack'll be fine in a minute, won't you, Zack." He pulled his friend over to the chair and pushed him down. "Just sit there. I'll straighten this out."

"Mr. Beadlesberry, can we just go over there in the corner and talk about this?"

"Of course, polite Tyler Trent. Please, what is this word Mr. you use before my name. I am Bartholomew B. or Mayor Beadlesberry." The old man waded through the piles of books to a small table and cleared off two chairs. He sat down and folded his hands in his lap. Tyler glanced over at Zack, who seemed to be staring into space and occasionally shuddering. At least he had stopped yelling.

"Okay, so let's pretend that you don't know who we are and you never heard of New York City. Aren't you curious about us? I mean we don't dress like everybody else and we're taller. We don't even talk like the people here."

"Yes, well, that is true, young Tyler. You must come from the south. Someplace like Balowag."

Tyler closed his eyes for a second. "Balowag, right. Listen, I need to talk to my friend, I'll be right back." Tyler moved as fast as he could through the obstacle course of books and shook Zack's shoulder. "Hey, you okay?"

Zack nodded. His eyes were shiny. "I really want to go home, Tyler."

"I know, me too. But right now we have to find the pendant and this Beadlesberry doesn't even know who we are. He won't be able to help us."

Zack just stared up at Tyler, his eyes ready to overflow.

"I think we should go back to the inn and look for the pendant. Then we can come back here and try to get home," Tyler said.

Zack nodded again.

"Are you all right, Zack Vander?" Tyler jumped. Beadlesberry was right behind him. He wished the old man would stop sneaking around. Then he remembered, this was a different Beadlesberry, or was he really so different? Maybe he was lying. Tyler wondered if Beadlesberry thought they might be the young warriors of the legend. He might just stop them from going home.

Tyler took a chance. "Uh, Mr. Mayor, uh, Mayor Beadlesberry, do you think we're the young warriors in the legend of Maidenspa?"

Zack glared at Tyler, who put his finger across his lips and shook his head.

The old man's eyes glinted and his mouth became a narrow line. "One never knows. Strange things have been happening here. Then Tyler and Zack suddenly come to town. One might just speculate."

Speculate, speculate. Guessing? Tyler's brain whirled. Where was his Mom when he really needed her? "We're just twelve years old, Mr. Beadlesberry, we don't fight wizards or dragons."

The old man shrugged his bony shoulders. "As I said, just speculation about an unusual coincidence." Then he leaned closer, his beady eyes shining. "Or serendipity."

Tyler knew he would have to pay more attention in English, maybe even start reading the dictionary. He said, "We have to go now. There is something I must find. Will you be here later?"

"As I said before, one never knows," the old man grinned, sharp teeth poking out from his dark gums.

"Come on, Zack, let's get out of here." Tyler pulled his friend out the door and waited until it shut behind him. "Did you notice something weird about this Beadlesberry?"

Zack nodded. "I don't trust him."

"We didn't trust the other one either. I meant his personality. It's like he's got this mean look in his eyes and around his mouth," Tyler said. "You know I saw the same thing in Dismar's eyes for just a second yesterday. I don't trust him either."

Zack said, "I didn't see anything wrong."

"You weren't looking at him."

"Listen, Tyler, forget the mean eyes, wizards and dragons. We need that pendant." He looked toward the next shop. "No, right now I need chocolate."

Fine, Tyler thought, anything to keep him calm. He needed Zack to be thinking. "Chocolate. Okay. What do you think they use for money around here?"

Zack turned toward the confectionery. "Let's go in and find out."

"It looks like the gingerbread house in Hansel and Gretel," Tyler said. The front of the store was decorated in giant striped candy canes and gumdrops.

"I hope the wicked witch isn't inside," Zack said, his voice shaking.

The door looked like a giant candy bar. Tyler pushed a handle shaped like an enormous licorice stick. As he crossed the threshold, he thought he had stepped into chocolate heaven. The smell was everywhere.

"Look at this place," Zack said, his mouth hanging open. They stared at the shelves filled with candy. Tyler could feel his mouth filling up with water. Soon he would be drooling down the front of his tee shirt.

A bald head popped up from behind the counter. "Aha, my first customers. Welcome boys. You must be the young warriors from Balowag. I am Calamar, the confectioner, at your service. Young man, you need to wipe your mouth." He pointed at Tyler.

Tyler's face flamed. He pulled up the front of his shirt and wiped his lips.

"Nothing to be embarrassed about. It happens quite often. People just seem to lose control when surrounded by so much chocolate. So what can I do for you?"

"Um, we would like some candy, but we don't know if we have the right money," Zack said.

"What is money, young man?" Calamar asked.

Tyler fished in his pocket and pulled out a quarter and a dollar. "This is money. We use it to buy things."

Calamar took the quarter and felt the raised picture of George Washington. Then he reached for the dollar and looked at both sides. "Hmm, same man. He must be very important in Balowag."

Tyler tried not to smile. "Oh, yes, he was the first president."

"Ah, I did not know Balowagans had presidents. We just have a mayor. Beadlesberry you know. He has always been the mayor," Calamar said.

"Always? Does that mean forever?" Zack asked.

"Oh yes. Beadlesberry is very old. Ancient you might say," Calamar stated seriously.

"You mean he's immortal?" Tyler asked.

"Of course. Someone has to be. Otherwise how would we know history?" Calamar leaned across the counter. "Now what can I get you boys?"

Tyler knew exactly how Alice had felt as she tried to make sense of the doormouse. Just play along. "We can't pay you."

Calamar leaned across the counter until his face was just inches from the boys. His brown eyes gleamed. He looked at each boy in turn. "Oh, we do not pay for things around here with what you call money. You will pay me someday for the candy. Yes indeed, when I call upon you, you will pay."

Tyler wasn't sure he liked the sound of that. What kind of payment would Calamar expect from them? Then he realized that with luck they wouldn't be here long enough for Calamar to collect the debt. "I'll have a bag of turtles and some licorice, please."

Calamar turned to Zack. "And you, quiet one, what confection will you eat today?"

"Jelly beans and chocolate covered peanuts," Zack said.

Calamar handed each boy a small chocolate bar covered with coconut. "Special treat for the first customers of the day." Then he began to scoop candy and dropped it into small bags. Suddenly he said, "So young warriors have you figured out who among us is the Wizard of Maidenspa?"

Tyler and Zack each choked on a mouthful of candy. "Bmfphug," Tyler mumbled through the coconut stuck to his teeth.

"Excellent, you have so many to choose from. It will be a grand exercise for your brains. Yes indeed." He tied each bag with a ribbon and handed them across the counter. His voice deepened. "Be very, very careful, young warriors. Wizards can be very dangerous."

He came around the counter and opened the door. With a sweep of his arm he gestured them out of the store. "Good bye young warriors. We shall meet again." Goose bumps rose on Tyler's arms as he squeezed by Calamar. The door slammed behind them.

"What was that all about?" Zack asked, as he untied one of the bags.

Tyler shrugged. "I don't know. I just wish the whole town didn't think we were the warriors of the legend."

"Yeah, I don't have much experience fighting wizards," Zack said, popping a jellybean in his mouth.

"Did you notice his eyes gleam when he was talking to us?" Tyler asked.

"You see evil eyes everywhere." Tyler gave him a dirty look and started across the street. "Where are you going?" Zack called as he hurried to catch up.

"I just don't want to walk past the apothecary or the bookshop again," Tyler said.

"Don't worry about the bookstore, Tyler. It's gone again."

Tyler looked back and there was an empty space between the confectionery and the apothecary. A large black bird sat on the edge of the roof of the apothecary watching him. What are you looking at, he thought. Then he shook his head and sighed. Some adventure. He hoped he would be able to find the pendant back at the Inn, or they were in big trouble.

Tyler wondered what his parents were doing right now. Did they call the police, or maybe the FBI? He was sure his mother knew by now that he had never gone to a local bookstore. There was a pressure in his chest and his eyes filled with tears. He wanted to feel his mother's arms around him again.

Tyler gritted his teeth. If he ever got back, he would never speak to Uncle Tad again. In fact, he would tell his parents just whose fault it was. They would never speak to Uncle Tad again. Maybe Uncle Tad would get eaten by a giant octopus and never come back. It would serve him right.

Tyler clenched his fists and dug his nails into his palms. Stupid, stupid, stupid. Why did he ever listen to his Uncle? And then to drag Zack along. More stupid. Tyler wanted to cry, run, scream and punch out somebody at the same time. He shoved a huge chocolate turtle into his mouth and chomped down on the peanuts. He chewed faster as he practically ran down the road. Find the pendant, find the pendant, find the pendant.

High in the sky the large black bird followed them.

Chapter 11

Woofens and Purrens

Tyler was breathing hard by the time they reached the lake. He could hear Zack panting behind him. “Hey wait up, Tyler,” Zack called. The steam cloud rising from the lake was lower now and the bubbles were small pops on the surface. “I guess it’s cooling down,” Zack puffed, catching up.

"Just simmering, we say."

The boys whirled. A giant stood there grinning, a long, sharp scythe in his huge hands. They stepped back quickly. He shifted the scythe to one hand and held up an arm the size of a small tree trunk. "Name is Bramble. I bet you boys are brave warriors from Balowag." They nodded, moving further back. He retracted his arm. "No need to fear old Bramble. Quite harmless. Just one of the giant people from the North." Then he turned back toward the woods, swinging the scythe in a rhythmic swish, swish across the grass.

Both boys exhaled at the same time. "Man, I thought we were goners for sure," Zack said.

"This place just gets weirder and weirder. Do you feel like you fell down a rabbit hole and through a looking glass?" Tyler said.

Zack slapped Tyler on the back. "You know, pal, you gotta to stop hanging around the house so much. Your Mom's rubbing off on you." Then he danced away. "Next thing you know you'll be teaching English literature at some fancy school, quoting dead people all the time."

Tyler hooked his fingers, stepping menacingly toward his friend. "I want to make your flesh creep.”

“Yuck, who said that?” Zack laughed, backing up.

Tyler shrugged. “I don’t know. Somebody dead. I’ll ask my mother.” Tyler realized what he had just said and stared down at his shoes. Would he ever see his mother again? Even Uncle Tad would look good right now. The boys stood there quietly listening to the distant swish of the scythe.

Then Zack broke the silence. “Do you wonder how they do it?”

“How who does what?” Tyler asked.

“You know,” Zack said. “Crumble is so tiny and Bramble is a giant. I mean she’s not really tiny, not like Ellaby or Esmara, but she sure is small compared to Bramble.”

Tyler smacked the side of his head. “I can’t believe it. Is that all you can think about? We’re stuck in Never Never Land with a bunch of loonies who think there are dragons breathing fire because some wizard put a spell on it or something and all you can think about is sex.”

Zack shrugged. “It’s not all I ever think about. It’s just…you know? I mean…oh, never mind. Forget I said anything.” Tyler smirked.

They circled the lake and heard Pottaby yapping and Ellaby calling him. When they cleared the mist, Tyler could see her carrying a wicker basket filled that overflowed with bed linens and towels. “Hello,” she said when they were closer. “Just hanging up the laundry.

“Did you just wash all that? Is it from our room?” Tyler asked.

Ellaby nodded. “Actually Crumble did the washing, I am just helping her hang the linens. Is something wrong?”

Tyler tried to be calm. “I had a gold pendant that I seem to have lost last night. I just wondered if you found it when you stripped the bed.”

“There was nothing like that in the room. I checked very carefully,” she said. “Was it valuable?”

“Well, yes,” Tyler said, hesitating. “Uh, my Uncle Tad had it as a kid. It means a lot,”

Zack turned and looked at Tyler, who shrugged. A small lie was better than the truth. Anyway, if it hadn’t been for his Uncle he would never have gone to the bookstore in the first place and then he wouldn’t have the pendant. Besides, his Uncle Tad did have it as a kid or he wouldn’t have gone to King Arthur’s Court and come back. That’s supposing Beadlesberry was telling the truth in the first place. Man, this was so complicated.

“Oh, I am sorry. Let me hang the clothes and then I will help you look for it.” Ellaby turned toward the back of the building.

Tyler said, “Hey, don’t worry about it, we’ll just go upstairs and check around. Come on Zack.”

The boys looked behind, under and in the furniture. They looked in the bathroom. Pottaby sat

nearby wagging his tail, his head cocked to one side. Tyler looked down at him. “Did you see a gold pendant, boy?”

“Woof.”

“Guess not,” Tyler said, patting the top of his head.

Zack pulled all the clean bedding off and they turned over the mattress. “Ellaby’s gonna kill us,” Zack said, trying to put the sheet back on.

"Never mind Ellaby, Crumble's the one to watch out for," Tyler said, pushing the mattress back into the middle of the bed.

"What are you doing?" A loud voice resounded in the doorway.

The boys dropped the bedding and backed toward the window. "Um, we're sorry, Crumble." Tyler said meekly. "I lost something valuable and I was just trying…."

"Humph, let me do that,” Crumble said, yanking the sheets from the bed and dropping them on the floor.

Ellaby peered in the door. “I told you it was not in the bed. Crumble would have given it to me if she had found it.”

“Hey, sorry, but I had to check anyway,” Tyler said.

Ellaby pushed him away and helped Crumble remake the bed. Then she stood in the middle of the room, hands on her hips. “Did you wear it to bed last night?”

Tyler nodded. “I never took anything off, well except my shoes. Then there was the earthquake or whatever that was and we ran downstairs.”

“Maybe the ribbon broke while you were sleeping and it fell out of your shirt this morning,” Ellaby suggested.

They all ran down the stairs, Pottaby barking and leaping after them. They crawled around on their hands and knees searching every inch of grass. No pendant. Finally, Ellaby stood. “I have work to do. It is not easy being an innkeeper's daughter. I will come back later.”

“Thanks for trying. I’m sorry about the bed,” Tyler said.

Ellaby shrugged and turned away. Then she turned back and smiled. “I am never angry very long.” Tyler watched her walk away.

“Did you see that dimple when she smiled?” Zack asked.

“Shut up and keep looking,” Tyler growled.

Zack laughed. Pottaby stretched out on a sunny patch of grass and put his head on his front paws. He watched the boys crawl around for the next half hour, poking through the grass. At last they had covered every blade of grass and fell on their backs next to the dog. Hoping for a belly scratch, Pottaby rolled onto his back and stuck his four paws up in the air. Zack reached over and obliged the dog. Pottaby sighed and closed his eyes.

"Right now, I wish I was a dog and could just lie here in the sun without a care in the world," Zack said.

"With somebody scratching you belly?" Tyler said.

"Depends on who," Zack said dreamily.

"Oh, like Julie Bateman?" Tyler asked.

"Sounds good to me," Zack mumbled.

Tyler poked Zack in the ribs. "Don't fall asleep. If we don't find the pendant you'll never see Julie Bateman again, or anyone else we know."

Zack sat up. "Right. Let's look in the dining room. Maybe it fell off when we were eating breakfast."

Pottaby grunted and rolled over on his side. The boys jumped up and ran into the house. Pottaby just looked up and then went back to sleep. They looked under the dining room table and under the seat cushions on the chairs. Zack checked every pitcher and bowl on the table. Tyler checked all the corners and under the sideboard. No pendant. They looked at each other and said, "The garbage."

They ran in the kitchen and looked around. "Where do people in the country keep the garbage? They don't have an incinerator room." Tyler said.

"Out, out of my kitchen," Crumble roared from the dining room door.

"Let's try outside," Zack said. They found two wooden barrels of garbage to the right of the rear door.

"We'll each take one," Tyler said.

"Yuck, this is disgusting," Zack said, rummaging through the barrel. "Soggy pancakes. Look, black eggs. I told you so. This is probably why the pancakes were white." He held up an eggshell that dripped white slime."

"Looks like snot," Tyler said.

"Vampire spit," Zack suggested.

"I thought that was black," Tyler said, holding up the rind from a flyfruit.

Zack said, "Depends what book you read." Tyler didn't answer. Zack turned to look at his friend. Tyler was holding a black ribbon in his hand. "Hey, you found it."

Tyler shook his head. "Just the ribbon. See the knot is open and the pendant is missing." He dangled it to its full length.

Zack shoved all the garbage back in his barrel and grabbed Tyler's barrel. He turned it over and all the garbage fell out on the ground. The two boys rooted around in the wet sloppy mess but there was no gold pendant.

Then they turned over the other barrel and did the same thing again. No gold pendant.

"What are you boys doing?" Dunby said loudly. "Look at this mess."

Tyler looked up. "Listen, sir, we're really sorry. We'll clean it all up."

"I have never had guests who went through the garbage or unmade their beds." Dunby pushed his hands through his hair. It stood up straight.

Ellaby came around the corner. She covered her mouth, but Tyler could see her shoulders shaking. She grabbed her father with her free hand and pulled him down. Then she whispered in his ear. Dunby started laughing. Tyler wondered just what she had told him.

"All right, young warriors. Just be sure and clean up after you finish looking for usable leftovers." Dunby turned and walked off. They could hear his laughter grow fainter.

"What did you say to him?" Tyler asked.

"Well, Tyler Trent, I told him it was a Balowagan tradition. Balowagans had to make sure there were no usable leftovers after each meal. Something about being very thrifty." Ellaby giggled.

Tyler couldn't help smiling. Ellaby sounded like his mother's wind chimes, which he would probably never hear again unless they found the pendant. "We found the ribbon but the pendant isn't in here. I just don't know where to look anymore."

"I will help you after I finish hanging the clothes," Ellaby offered.

"Maybe we can help you," Zack offered.

Ellaby grabbed the basket back. "Oh no, guests never help. You just rest on the porch and I will return soon. You can talk to Pottaby."

Zack sat on the top step. "So what's the plan?"

Tyler climbed the porch stairs and sat down next to him. "We have to find the pendant."

"I know that," Zack said. "How do we find the pendant?"

"Leave me alone, I need to think." Tyler cupped his hands around his chin and rested them on his knees. "Just need time to think."

"Yeah, well think fast, it's getting late. I really don't want to spend another night here." Zack said.

Pottaby spun around in circles and then rolled onto his back, feet in the air. Zack reached behind him and absently rubbed the dog's belly.

They sat in silence listening to the birds and the distant swish of the scythe. Tyler caught movement out of the corner of his eye. He turned and there was the black bird sitting on the porch railing. He nudged Zack, "Look, over there." Zack turned just as the bird lifted into the blue sky, beating its wings. "Did you see it?" Tyler asked.

"What, the bird?" Tyler nodded. "So what." Zack shrugged. "Just a crow or a raven or something."

"Well, I think it's following us," Tyler said.

"Right, a big black raven is following us. You know, you're spooked, man. Better get a grip before you lose it totally," Zack said. Tyler didn't answer. He tried to count the number of times he had seen the bird, but gave up. Maybe he was losing it.

"All right, Tyler and Zack, let us find your missing pendant."

Tyler jumped. "You scared me. Ellaby laughed her tinkly laugh and sat on the other side of Tyler. "Perhaps you lost it last night on the stairway to nowhere."

Tyler stared at her. "How did you know?"

"Pottaby told me," she said.

Zack looked at Pottaby strangely. "He's a dog, how could he tell you anything?"

"What is a dog?" Ellaby asked.

"Uh, never mind," Zack said quickly. "So Pottaby can talk?"

"Well, yes. Of course he doesn't talk our language, but if you know woofish you can speak to him." Ellaby picked up Pottaby and said something unintelligible. Pottaby wagged his tail and smiled.

Tyler jumped up, pointing to the dog. "He smiled, I saw him smile" He turned to Zack. "Did you see that, he smiled."

Zack turned away. "I didn't see a thing. Dogs don't smile."

Ellaby pouted. "What is this word, dog, you keep using. Is that what they call woofens in Balowag?"

"Uh, right, dogs," Zack said. "And um, cats, they like purr."

Tyler turned away so Ellaby wouldn't see his grin.

Ellaby said, "Of course, purrens. Drumthwack the keeper of the debts has a pink long-haired purren, named Kittythwack. We don't see many purrens around here."

Zack looked across at Tyler and mouthed. "Purrens."

Tyler and Zack burst out laughing. Tyler bent over double, his shoulders shaking. Zack fell back on the porch, clutching his stomach.

Ellaby shook her head and murmured in Pottaby's ear. The woofen made some sounds deep in his throat. Crumble came out onto the porch.

"Are they ill?" Crumble knelt down and felt Zack's forehead.

Ellaby jumped up. "I don't think so, Crum. They just aren't used to hearing woofish. There are only dogs and purrens in Balowag."

"Ah, then they should meet Kittythwack. They will feel right at home," she said. "Lunch is ready, lumpas and zoggs."

The boys looked at each other and laughed harder. Ellaby carried Pottaby into the house leaving them on the porch. "Help, I can't breathe," Zack gasped.

"Kittythwack?" Tyler started laughing again. It took a while until they were able to speak.

Zack had hiccups. "Lumpas, hic, and zoggs?"

"Wouldn't it be nice if Crumble meant hamburgers and fries?" Tyler asked.

"I wouldn't count on it, hic," Zack said. Tyler smacked him in the middle of the back, but Zack continued to hiccup all the way into the dining room.

Chapter 12

Pottaby's Treasure

Ellaby was seated at the table when the boys came into the dining room and sat down opposite her. "I thought I would join you for lunch. Before he left, Papa said it was all right. I do not meet many young people living all the way out here by Maidenspa."

"Great," Tyler said, grinning. Zack nudged him in the ribs. Tyler kicked him under the table. "Where is your father?"

"He had to go away for a while with some of the townsmen," Ellaby said quietly. "Don't you have any friends?" he asked.

"Yes, of course. There are Lisamara and Dellthwacky and Lisamara's twin brother Dismar the younger." Ellaby said.

"I don't remember seeing any kids with Dismar and Esmara yesterday," Zack said, pouring a glass of what he guessed was milk.

"They were there, just not with their parents. Everyone in Balalac was at the lake yesterday. It was a very important town meeting. Mayor Beadlesberry told everyone his decision."

Crumble entered carrying a tray of food. Tyler eyed the platters warily and then brightened. It was burgers and fries, well almost. He thought the burgers looked more like dog turds. He looked across at Ellaby and asked, "What decision?"

"Oh, his decision to bring Gruen, the dragon hunter, to Maidenspa," Ellaby said.

"Eat!" Crumble ordered, pointing at Zack.

"Yes, ma'am," Zack said quickly, helping himself to some of the food.

Tyler watched Zack gingerly poke the patty with his fork.

"You, eat!" Crumble wagged a finger at Tyler. "Got to fatten you up, boy. Cannot have skinny warriors fighting wizards and dragons. Besides, if you finish this, you will have pink putty for dessert." She turned and marched into the kitchen.

Pink putty? Then Tyler remembered her giant husband swinging his scythe and reached for his fork. Ellaby giggled. "Do not mind Crumble, she loves children. She and Bramble have never been able to have any of their own, so she takes care of everyone else's children. She has been caring for me since I was born, and my mother before me."

Tyler looked across the table. "Um, I was wondering. Where is your mother?"

A shadow of sadness crossed her face. "She went to the bookshop and never returned."

Zack gulped. "What do you mean, she never returned. She just disappeared?"

Ellaby nodded. "We searched and searched, but never found her."

"Did you ask Beadlesberry? I mean did she ever get to the bookshop?" Zack asked.

Ellaby shook her head. "The bookshop disappeared for several days and when it returned, Mayor Beadlesberry said he was sorry but Mama had never reached his store."

"That's so terrible. I'm sorry, Ellaby," Tyler said. "When did this happen?"

"About one month ago," Ellaby said. A tear dropped from her eyelid. She swiped at it with her hand and sniffed. "Papa has gone again to look for her."

Tyler wondered how anyone could disappear in a place as small as Balalac, where everybody knew everybody. Maybe she hitched a ride like they did and got kidnapped or murdered. Get real; this wasn't New York with serial killers and murderers. There were only wizards and dragons. Maybe she found out about the wizard and he cast a spell on her. Tyler wondered if there was some connection to what was happening now at Maidenspa. "Hey, we didn't mean to make you sad," Tyler said quickly.

"I am sorry. You are guests in the Inn. I should not be telling you sad things," Ellaby said, forcing a smile. "Let us finish eating. You will love pink putty."

Tyler heard Zack mumble, "Wonder if it's anything like silly putty?" Tyler grinned.

Ellaby asked, "What is silly putty, Zack Vander?"

"Oops," Zack said. "Um…."

"It's very stretchy, like taffy," Tyler said.

"Ah, a confection. Perhaps Calamar has some of this silly putty. He can probably order some from Balowag for you," Ellaby suggested.

Tyler changed the subject. "So tell us about Calamar."

Ellaby seemed relieved to talk about something else. "Of course. Calamar is descended from a long line of confectioners. His father and grandfather and his father before him were confectioners. He has a soft spot in his heart for children, always giving away free candy. Do you not just love the way he has decorated his store? Just like a gingerbread house."

"I thought his family would have been apothecaries, like Dismar," Tyler said.

"Dismar's family have all been apothecaries. They are cousins. Their mothers were sisters. They are very different though," Ellaby explained.

"Different?" Zack asked.

Ellaby continued. "Dismar can be dark sometimes. Perhaps it is working with chemicals and compounds all day. Perhaps it is always giving things to people who are sick or hurt. Calamar is fun and happy like his confections."

Tyler nodded. Maybe Ellaby only saw one side of Calamar or maybe he was getting paranoid, seeing evil in everybody. "Tell me about the Mayor. Calamar says he is immortal."

"Immortal. Does that mean forever?" Ellaby was about to continue when Crumble came in with three bowls of something smooth and creamy.

Ellaby giggled. "You boys are funny. Are they not, Crum? It is just putty."

Crumble nodded. "There is more if you want it. POTTABY, OUT!" The boys jumped. Crumble pointed at the dog sneaking under the table. "There will by no woofen in my dining room spraying fur all over the place." Tyler watched the little polka-dot creature slink away, tail between his legs. Pottaby turned around and sat in the doorway watching them. Tyler could swear he winked at him. Man, he was losing it.

"Pink putty for everyone." She placed the bowls in front of each of them and then stood back, arms crossed over her chest, smiling.

Zack, always ready to try anything labeled dessert, even if it wasn't pink, but ugly gray, dipped his spoon into the dish and licked the tip. "Oh man, oh man, ice cream."

Zack hadn't barfed or fallen over dead, so Tyler decided it was safe to taste the glop. "Nope, pudding," he exclaimed, licking his lips.

"Poor Pottaby," Ellaby said. "Crumble is always chasing him out of some room or another. Then she feeds him lumpas. He loves her."

Zack said, "I know, he told you, right?"

Ellaby nodded. "Of course. Pottaby tells me everything." She ate a spoonful of putty and then said, "You asked me about the Mayor. He is a forever person, at least that is what he has told everyone. He knows everything about the history of Balalac, even before the healing waters of Maidenspa."

"Couldn't he have learned that from books and asking questions?" Tyler asked.

"Oh no, the things he knows are not in any books. He is a forever person."

"I'm stuffed." Zack pushed his plate away and sat back. "Ellaby, why does the bookshop disappear like that, and where is Beadlesberry while it's gone?"

Ellaby thought carefully before answering. "We do not really know where the store goes when it disappears. It just is not there any more. Beadlesberry is just gone too. No one has ever asked him, either. The town believes he is some kind of magician and we are a bit afraid of him."

"I can understand how you could feel that way. He is kind of scary." Tyler said.

"Do you think he might be the wizard?" Zack asked.

"Nobody believes that. He has been around forever. Nothing like this has ever happened before. I think he is just a magic person who likes travel. People from south and the giants of the north say the bookshop sometimes appears in their towns and then goes away again. Perhaps he visits other places when he is not in Balalac."

Zack looked at Tyler and raised his eyebrows. "You mean like New York."

Ellaby wrinkled her forehead. "What is New York?"

Tyler frowned at Zack and said, "Just a place in the south, near Balowag."

"I have never heard of this place New York," Ellaby said. "Tell me about it. Is it like Balalac?"

"Uh, uh," Tyler said. "It's mostly gray, with lots of stone buildings and glass."

"Not many trees, either. The buildings are really tall," Zack added.

"It sounds depressing," Ellaby said.

“Sometimes, but then there is always something exciting happening in New York.” Tyler said.

“It does not sound at all like Balalac. How can people be content without happy trees and flowers? What could be more exciting than the popp picking contest or the flyfruit bakeoff during the fruit festival? Ellaby’s shoulders quivered with delight. “Last year Crumble won first place for her flyfruit upside down cake.”

Tyler knew that if he didn’t leave the table right then and there, he would embarrass everyone by having hysterics. “Gotta go, um, quick.” He jumped up and rushed out of the dining room and up the stairs to his room. He fell on the bed laughing. He finally calmed down enough to take in big gulps of air. His side hurt from laughing so hard. The bed bounced as Pottaby jumped up.

Tyler turned toward the dog. “Woof,” he gasped. “Woof, woof.” Then he fell back again laughing harder. Pottaby put his front paws on Tyler’s chest and breathed into his face.

Tyler suddenly stopped laughing. This wasn’t funny at all. Why was he laughing at a flyfruit bakeoff or a berry-picking contest? He should have learned by now that people found lots of different ways to have fun. He wasn’t the son of an archeologist for nothing. Maybe Ellaby would find a light show at the planetarium boring.

Pottaby sat back and nodded his head. Tyler sat up. Pottaby nodded his head. He understood everything Tyler was thinking. Maybe woofens were like dolphins, intelligent animals with their own language that we just didn’t understand. Well, maybe he didn’t understand woofen, but Ellaby seemed to be able to communicate with Pottaby. Tyler wondered if everyone in Maidenspa could talk with woofens or just Ellaby.

Pottaby reached out a paw and tapped Tyler’s hand. Tyler opened his hand and stretched it toward Pottaby. The little woofen opened his mouth and dropped something into it. Tyler looked down. At first he thought Pottaby given him the pendant, but it was a small, shiny silver key. “Thank you Pottaby, but this is not what I need. I wish you could talk to me. I bet you know where the pendant is.”

Pottaby woofed again and tapped Tylers hand with his paw. “Wait a minute, does this key have something to do with the pendant?”

Pottaby woofed twice. “All right, now we’re getting somewhere. Does the key fit something like a door or a box? Is the pendant inside whatever the key fits?”

Pottaby woofed again. "Man, this is like a game of twenty questions, but I don't understand the answers," Tyler said, pulling at his hair. Okay, calm down. Let's take this slow and easy, one question at a time.

"Now, Pottaby, woof once for yes and twice for no, okay?" Pottaby nodded. Tyler glanced around. He was glad nobody was around to see this. Back home they would lock him away for talking to a dog.

"Hey, you okay?" Zack said from the doorway.

"Get in here and shut the door, quick," Tyler said.

"Okay, okay, calm down." Zack shut the door behind him and sat on the edge of the bed. "So what's going on? It sounded like you were talking to the dog."

"First of all it's not a dog, it's a woofen." Pottaby woofed once. Tyler grinned. "Yes, see he said yes."

"Sure he did," Zack said skeptically.

"Just listen, okay? He came in here and gave me this silver key. Then I started asking him questions real fast and he started woofing. He's trying to communicate, you know like dolphins whistle, well woofens woof."

Zack sat back. "So let's hear it."

"Fine. Now we agreed that one woof means yes and two woofs means no."

"Who agreed, you and Pottaby?" Zack asked, grinning.

"You're being a jerk. Don't interrupt, just listen. Can you do that?" Tyler was frustrated and getting angry.

"Okay, okay, don't get mad," Zack said. Tyler was mean when he got mad.

Tyler took a deep breath and closed his eyes. Think calm. He breathed in and out. When he was in control again he said, "Pottaby, does the key fit a door?"

"Woof, woof."

"Does the key fit a box?"

"Woof."

"Okay, great." Tyler was getting excited. "Um, is the pendant in the box?"

"Woof, woof"

"Hey, this is terrific," Zack said, jumping up and down. "He's really talking to you."

"Two means no, Zack. Just shut up, I don't want to lose track." Tyler turned to the dog again. “Pottaby, do you know what’s in the box?”

“Woof.”

“Fantastic. So can you take us to it?”

“Woof, woof.”

“Well if you know where it is, why can’t you take us there?” Tyler asked.

Pottaby just stared at him, tongue hanging out.

Tyler rolled his eyes. “Dummy, he can only answer yes or no. Okay, let’s start again. Is the box someplace that disappeared?”

Pottaby tail wagged. “Woof.”

Zack interrupted. “Can I ask a question?”

Pottaby woofed once.

Zack grinned. “All right, Pottaby. Is it behind the disappearing door that leads to the stairway to nowhere?”

“Woof.”

Zack slapped his hand against Tyler’s and they both grinned. “Now we’re getting somewhere,” he said.

Tyler shook his head. “I don’t see that we’re getting anywhere. The door disappeared last night, remember? The stairway goes nowhere. It was black in there. They don’t have flashlights. Even if the door reappeared, what happens if it disappears again before we can get the pendant and escape?”

“Woof, woof, woof.”

Two heads turned toward the woofen. “What do three woofs mean?” Tyler asked.

Zack shrugged. “Beats me, man.”

“Maybe we should tell Ellaby everything. She can communicate with Pottaby. I don’t know how else to find the answer.” Tyler hung his head. Pottaby pushed against Tyler’s face and licked his nose. Tyler put his arms around Pottaby and hugged him. “You tried boy, you really tried. I just don’t speak woofen.”

Zack looked up, tears filling the corners of his eyes. “Listen, Tyler, I’m willing to try anything. I really want to get home. Like, why don’t we take a chance. Ellaby seems nice. I don’t think she’s a wizard.”

Tyler frowned. “Of course she’s not a wizard or wizardess or whatever. She just talks to animals. Pottaby, should we tell Ellaby everything?”

“Woof.”

Tyler shrugged. “Okay, I guess that’s the answer.” He didn’t believe he was taking advice from a dog or woofen or whatever. Tyler tucked the key in his pocket and the two boys, with Pottaby dancing around their feet, went in search of Ellaby. There was a rustle of leaves in the tree overhead. Tyler looked up and there was the raven looking down on them. Tyler grabbed Zack's sleeve and pointed. "It's back again."

"I hope it isn't supposed to be bad luck or something," Zack said.

"My Dad once said some Native Americans believe the raven's a trickster," Tyler said.

"Great," Zack moaned. "Now the birds are weird. How can we believe anything around here?"

"Come on," Tyler pulled him along. They found Ellaby helping Bramble weed the vegetable garden. "Um, Ellaby, can we talk to you for a few minutes?" Tyler asked.

Pottaby woofed several times and Ellaby stood up, smiling. "I see you have been discussing things with Pottaby." She kissed Bramble on the cheek and led the way toward the lake. The giant sat back on his heels and watched them walk away.

The orange sun inched its way toward the horizon, blurred by steam rising from the cooling water of the lake. Ellaby sighed and sat down on the grass. "It used to be so beautiful here during the sunset. People would gather every night for picnic suppers. If only the dragon would stop breathing fire, things would go back to the way they were before the wizard cast his spell."

Tyler scratched his head. This wasn't going to be easy. "Ellaby, listen I know you have a really terrible problem here at Maidenspa, but Zack and me, we have a really awful problem. We can't get home."

Ellaby looked at Zack and then Tyler. "I know. First you have to solve our problem, then you will be able to go home."

"What are you talking about?" Zack said.

"You know the story of the young warriors who will unmask the wizard and remove the spell from the dragon and restore the lake," Ellaby explained patiently.

Tyler gritted his teeth. "Why does everybody think we are these warriors?"

Ellaby shrugged. "Because you are."

Tyler jumped up and started pacing. "The only thing I know is we're not wizard-fighting warriors. We're a couple of twelve-year old kids from New York who got lost in some magical story, where we lost the pendant to get us back home."

"You are the warriors," Ellaby stubbornly insisted.

Tyler stopped and leaned over her, yelling, "We are not warriors."

Ellaby looked up at him and smiled. "There is no need to get so excited, Tyler Trent. It is very simple. First we must figure out who is the wizard."

"What do you mean 'we'? There is no 'we'. If you want to go on a wizard hunt, fine, but leave us out of it," Tyler shouted.

Zack stood up and put his hand on Tyler's shoulder. "Listen man, this isn't getting us anywhere. Why don't we just agree to disagree, okay?"

Tyler took a deep breath. "Fine, Zack, why don't you tell her the whole story." He sat down again.

Zack sat down too and told Ellaby the story of how they got to Balalac, the lost pendant and Tyler's conversation with Pottaby. When he finished they all sat in silence. Finally, Pottaby woofed and Ellaby leaned forward to listen to him. She spoke softly to him and he nodded his head, tiny ears flopping.

"Pottaby says all of this is connected, the missing pendant, the wizard and the dragon. He says we will get you home, but first you must help us. Are you willing to work together?" Ellaby asked.

Tyler started to speak, but Zack grabbed his arm and said, "Yeah."

Tyler hesitated, and then he nodded. "Okay."

"Excellent," Ellaby said.

"Woof."

Chapter 13

The Great Plan

After a tasty dinner of something unpronounceable, they sat on the porch and made a plan. Tyler listed the names of everyone in town who might be the wizard.

Topping the list was Dismar, then Calamar, and finally Beadlesberry. Ellaby insisted that His Honor the Mayor couldn't possible be a wizard, but Tyler put his name there anyway. He wouldn't put it past the skinny old man to set up this whole scenario just to trap them into playing at warriors. He didn't trust Beadlesberry at all. Especially since he was probably some kind of magician anyway. It wasn't much of a step from magician to wizard.

They needed information. Zack suggested that the next afternoon, they go into town and watch the suspects. "Like a stakeout."

"A what?" Ellaby asked.

"We wait around and when they leave we follow them," Zack explained. "Nothing happens until after dark anyway."

"We cannot be wandering around after dark," Ellaby said. "It is not safe."

Tyler disagreed. "I don't think there is a dragon wandering around in the woods. Someone would have seen it by now. I think it's in a cave somewhere, maybe underground."

"Impossible," Ellaby insisted.

"So you stay home," Zack said. "We'll go by ourselves."

Ellaby pressed her lips together. "You are not leaving me behind. I will go to the apothecary for some herbs. I will tell him that Crumble has suddenly started sniffling and needs some sneezeweed for tea. Then I will engage him in a conversation about dragons."

"That covers Dismar." Zack said. "I think I should visit Calamar."

Tyler shook his head. "You would pick him." Then he smiled at Ellaby. “Zack has a sweet tooth.” Ellaby raised her eyebrows. “Um, he loves anything with sugar,” Tyler explained.

Ellaby returned the smile. Tyler stared at the dimple in her chin. “And you, Tyler Trent? I suppose you will visit the bookshop.”

Tyler forced his eyes away from her chin and up to her eyes. They sparkled like his mother’s blue-white diamond ring. He held her eyes for a moment until Zack punched him on the arm. “Wake up, Tyler.”

Tyler jerked his arm and looked impatiently at Zack. “Yeah, I’ll talk to Beadlesberry, if he’s there.”

Zack nodded and turned to Ellaby. “Okay. Now, is there anyone else who could be the wizard? What about this Drumthwack person? You said he was the keeper of the debts. What’s that?”

“He keeps a record of who owes who in payment for what,” Ellaby said.

“You mean he’s like a banker,” Tyler said.

“I do not know this word banker. Is that a word from New York?” Ellaby asked.

“Yeah,” Tyler said. “He’s someone who keeps track of debts and holds payments until they can go to the person you owe.”

“Ah, exactly.” Ellaby said, clapping her hands. “Drumthwack keeps a record and then sends you a note telling what you owe in return for what you got.”

Zack asked, “So then you have to figure out how to pay back what you owe, right?”

Ellaby nodded. Then Tyler said, “We owe you for staying at the Inn and we owe Calamar for candy. Will we get a note telling us to repay these debts?”

“Tyler and Zack do not owe anyone in Maidenspa. You will find the wizard and destroy the dragon and Maidenspa will be restored. That will be payment enough.”

“Great,” Zack said somberly. “I’m never eating candy again.”

“Oh sure, this I have to see,” Tyler said, laughing. Ellaby’s giggle tinkled across the porch and into the darkening night.

“I won’t live long enough,” Zack sighed.

Ellaby patted Zack on the shoulder. “You are a brave warrior, Zack Vander. I am not at all worried. You should not worry either. Besides you will have Gruen, the Dragon Hunter to help you.”

Zack put his chin in his hands and sighed again. “Terrific. I don’t know why I was ever worried. You worried, Tyler?"

Tyler wasn't listening. He was thinking about the keeper of the debt. "We have to find a way to meet this Drumthwack. You said his daughter was your friend."

Ellaby said, "Well, she was until last winter. We had an interaction."

Tyler looked puzzled. "An interaction? You mean a fight?"

Ellaby nodded. "I really do not wish to discuss it. It was very unfortunate. She was most angry."

"Angry enough to tell her father?" Tyler asked.

Ellaby shrugged. "He would have found out anyway. I broke her nose. Do not look at me that way, Tyler Trent. It was an accident, but she is very vain about her face. She said I did it on purpose to make her ugly, so Dismar the Younger would like me and not her."

"How on earth could you have broken her nose by accident?" Tyler's voice rose.

"Hush, Tyler Trent. She accused me of trying to take Dismar the Younger away from her. She tried to pull my hair and fell over Pottaby flat on her face."

"I bet she said you told Pottaby to trip her," Zack said, trying to keep a straight face.

Ellaby nodded sadly. "Her nose was squashed flat."

Tyler turned away and put his hand over his mouth. He could see Zack out of the corner of his eye trying not to laugh. Suddenly, both boys let out a huge whoosh of air and doubled over laughing.

Ellaby jumped up, hands on hips. "You are both horrible. She was my best friend, until Pottaby squashed her nose." Then Ellaby sat down and started laughing too.

When they finally had themselves under control, Zack pointed at Pottaby innocently sleeping under the table and they began laughing again.

Wiping her eyes, Ellaby gasped, "Do you think Drumthwack did this because Dellthwacky and I had a fight."

"I don't know," Tyler said. Then he remembered the man and the girl he had bumped into the first day they came to Maidenspa. "Ellaby, do Drumthwack and Dellwacky have blond hair and are his eyes like dead black holes?"

"Yes, yes. Have you met them?"

He didn't answer her, but turned to Zack. "Do you remember the skinny man dressed all in red who yelled at us when we were trying to find

Beadlesberry? You know, when Beadlesberry was telling everybody about the dragon hunter. The man had these dead eyes and there was a girl with him who kept her hand over her face all the time."

"Yeah, I remember him. He called us young warriors and told us not to push," Zack said. "Was that Drumthwack?"

"Sounds like it," Tyler said. "I don't think he's going to speak to any of us."

Pottaby stood up and stretched. He peeked out from under the table and woofed.

"What was that, Pottaby?" Ellaby asked. They spoke in woofen for a few minutes and finally Ellaby jumped up and clapped her hands. "This is so wonderful. Pottaby will seek out Kittythwack. He says the purren does not like Drumthwack very much. Perhaps she will tell us what Drumthwack does in the evening."

Tyler grinned. "I didn't know you speak Purren too?"

"I do not, but Pottaby does," Ellaby said.

"Of course, I should have known." Tyler reached down and tickled Pottaby's ears. Pottaby smiled.

Ellaby stretched and yawned. "I am going to bed. See you at midnight."

Tyler glanced at his watch. It was ten thirty. "Why don't we just stay up? It isn't worth going to bed. Besides, who knows what we might see."

Zack peered into the darkness. "Fine as long as we stay right here on the porch next to the door."

"You're scared," Tyler said, smirking.

"Am not. Besides, I don't see you going off into the woods at night," Zack said. "Admit it, you're scared too."

Tyler didn't answer. Zack was right. He was scared. He wasn't sure what would happen tomorrow night. He wanted to be back in New York. Right now, he would rather take his chances alone on a deserted subway at three in the morning, to confronting a wizard and a dragon in the middle of the night. "Let's go inside and sit in my room," he suggested.

Zack's eyes brightened and the boys went upstairs. They sat on the edge of Tyler's bed. Finally, Zack yawned and lay back on the pillow. Tyler pinched himself to stay awake. He must have dozed off sitting up because the next time he looked at his watch, it was eleven fifty-eight. He shook Zack, who shot up like a jack-in-the-box. "What, what?"

"It's almost time for the earthquake. Let's go downstairs." Tyler headed for the door with Zack following close behind. They had just come to the dining room door when the ground began to shake. Ellaby appeared with Pottaby in her arms, followed by Crumble and Bramble.

They all sat on under the table waiting for the shaking to stop. Zack lay down and Pottaby snuggled next to him. "I think Pottaby likes you Zack," Ellaby said.

Zack yawned.

"He misses his dog, er woofen," Tyler said.

"I did not know you have a woofen, Zack. Is he in New, um, Balowag?" Ellaby corrected herself quickly.

"It's a she and her name is Scarlett," Zack said.

"Ah, a pretty name." Ellaby blushed.

"Right," Zack said. "She's an Irish Setter.

Bramble tried to follow the strange conversation. "What is an Irish Setter?"

Ellaby answered before Zack could speak, "Let me guess, it is a red woofen."

"A large red woofen, with lots of hair," Zack added.

"Pottaby was yellow before the color went away," Ellaby said, sadly.

"He'll be yellow again, Ellaby. Don't you worry," Zack said.

"I must visit Balowag one day. It sounds most interesting," Bramble said.

Tyler tuned out and listened to the sounds around them. Once he thought he heard the tree rustle, but it was too dark to see anything through the window. He was sure the bird was up there watching him. He pictured its eyes, like two black marbles glaring down at him. He could almost sense its presence. The tree rustled again and Tyler thought he heard the beating of wings. His hands were icy. He shivered and put them in his pockets.

In a while the ground stopped shaking and they trooped off to bed. Tyler stopped Zack in the hallway between their rooms. "Don't go looking for invisible doors and stairways to nowhere tonight. I gotta sleep, promise?"

Zack shrugged and went into his room, shutting the door. Pottaby stared at the door for a minute and then turned and followed Tyler. The boy left the door open a crack so Pottaby could go off and do his thing during the night and hopped into bed. He was so tired he fell asleep almost immediately.

The little woofen watched Tyler's chest rise and fall, then jumped off the bed and padded into the hallway. He sniffed Zack's door, then lay down between the boys' rooms. Pottaby put his head on his front paws and softly woofed. Nobody was going anywhere tonight.

Chapter 14

Gruen The Dragon Hunter

The next morning dawned dismal and cloudy. The lake bubbled and belched clouds of steam. After a breakfast of black eggs and fried zoggs, Tyler and Zack helped Bramble plant vegetable seeds and trim trees. The giant rarely spoke except to announce that the weather was good for planting seeds. Sometimes Tyler noticed him staring at them. He wondered if Bramble suspected what they were up to. If so, he never said anything. His longest sentence was "good weather, dig here, drop three seeds."

They didn't see Ellaby again until after a strange lunch of lumpy liquid that tasted like vegetable soup. Zack thought it looked like vomit. Tyler disagreed. "More like a toilet backing up."

"Disgusting," Zack said. Then he saw Crumble standing in the doorway, frowning. "Not the food, Crumble. It's delicious." He shoved a spoonful into his mouth.

Tyler grabbed his napkin and covered his mouth. "Mmm, yummy," he mumbled through the napkin.

Crumble nodded and turned back to the kitchen.

"Whew," Tyler whispered. "I don't know who makes me more nervous, Crumble or Bramble."

"I don't think my stomach is going to hold out much longer," Zack said. "I would give anything for some of my Mom's pot roast and mashed potatoes. I would even eat spinach."

Tyler laughed. "Watch what you ask for, Zack, you might get it."

"Hmm, right. Forget the spinach."

"I would give anything for pizza, double cheese, topped with pepperoni and onions. Man, my mouth is watering just thinking about it," Tyler said dreamily.

"Hey, you didn't notice a pizza parlor in town, did you?" Zack asked hopefully.

"Are you kidding?"

Zack frowned. "Just thought I'd ask."

"Ask what, Zack Vander?" Ellaby came in and sat down opposite the boys.

"Oh, there's a special food we have in New York called pizza and I was just wondering if you had anything like it in Balalac," Zack said. Ellaby shrugged, looking bewildered, so Zack described a pizza.

"I think perhaps Crum might be able to reproduce that food for you if it is something that will make you happy and content."

"Oh man, that would definitely go a long way to making me happy and content, other than finding the pendant and going home of course," he said.

Ellaby called Crumble into the dining room and the boys described a pizza. "I think that is possible, Tyler and Zack," she said. "Anything for the brave warriors. You did not seem to enjoy the soup. Bramble will accompany you to town to retrieve the necessary ingredients."

"You know we might not be coming right back, though. Ellaby wants to show us around," Tyler said.

"I will tell Bramble. You will return before dark, of course." Crumble looked carefully from one to the other. They all nodded. Crumble narrowed her eyes suspiciously and folded her arms across her chest. Tyler was sure she was reading their minds, just like his mother did, but she shrugged and said, "Just keep Pottaby away from the Drumthwack, Ellaby. You know he threatened to turn him into a purren."

"He can do that?" Zack asked.

Crumble shrugged. "Who knows. I certainly do not want purrens around this Inn. Their fur is worse than a woofen and they jump all over the furniture."

Pottaby looked up at Ellaby and woofed. She bent down and lifted him into her arms. "Do not worry, little woofen," she said. "No one is going to change you into a purren. Not while the brave warriors are around."

They could hear her calling Bramble from the back door. An hour later Bramble, the two brave warriors, and Ellaby headed through the mist toward town. Pottaby pranced in front of them.

The bookstore was standing between the apothecary and the confectionery. They said good-bye to Bramble and waited until he turned the corner. "Whew, that was close. I never thought he would leave," Tyler said.

"I'm off to see the candy man," Zack said.

Ellaby looked in the direction of the apothecary, "I shall acquire my herbs."

"We should all meet at the crossroads at five o'clock," Tyler said.

Ellaby leaned down and spoke to Pottaby, who woofed twice and padded down the street. He disappeared into a narrow alley.

"Is he gonna be all right?" Tyler asked.

"Pottaby is a very resourceful woofen. He will be fine. I just hope Kittythwack is prowling around outside today. However, I am sure Pottaby will find a way to get her out of the house." Ellaby smiled and kissed each boy before turning and crossing the street. "That is for luck."

Tyler touched his burning cheek. "Oh man, oh man."

"Yeah, fantastic," Zack murmered. He stared after her, his eyes glazed over.

Tyler punched his friend's arm. "Hey, wake up and don't get any ideas."

Zack grinned. "What're you gonna do, get Pottaby to break my nose?"

Tyler laughed until his eyes teared and his nose ran. He swiped his sleeve across his face.

"Yuck! Get it together, it's chocolate time." Zack headed across the street.

Tyler took in a shuddering breath and followed Zack. He hoped the bookshop would stay around long enough for him to get inside. Forget that, it had better not disappear while he was in there. Tyler pushed open the door and stepped across the threshold. The musty odor hit him immediately. There seemed to be even more books piled up around the store.

"Ah, it is valiant Tyler Trent, warrior extraordinaire." Beadlesberry appeared from behind a tall stack of books.

Tyler jumped. He wanted to kick himself. He should know by now that Beadlesberry would pop out somewhere. He opened his mouth but the old man cackled and said, "Of course, you are now in search of the wizard and you think I am he." Beadlesberry waggled his finger in Tyler's face. "Wrong, wrong, wrong. Not that I would not make a superb wizard, but I prefer the legerdemain of great magicians like Merlin."

Tyler had no idea what he was talking about. Beadlesberry leaned close enough to blow sour breath in Tyler's face. "I am not into enchantment, Tyler the unbeliever. I have the gift of clairvoyance and I can read the minds of fools, but I will not change you into a hairy toad. I have scruples."

Tyler was completely at a loss. He badly needed a dictionary or his mother.

"Um, Mayor Beadlesberry, if you are not the wizard then who is?"

Beadlesberry thin lips curled up. "Time you asked, young warrior. Come sit and have a glass of prickleberry juice." He reached behind him and produced two glasses of liquid. So now tell me what you and your friends have discovered."

Tyler wondered if he was giving away the game by telling Beadlesberry their plan. He needed to trust somebody and if Beadlesberry turned him into a hairy toad, well that was a chance he was going to take. Just as he was finishing the story, the door to the shop banged open.

A huge man stood in the doorway. He was at least eight feet or more with wide shoulders and muscles bulging underneath his striped shirt. Long hair hung down his back. His eyes were piercing, perched on either side of his large hooked nose. "I am Gruen, the dragon hunter. I seek His Honor, Bartholomew B. Beadlesberry," he boomed.

Beadlesberry lurched forward. Tyler was sure he would trip and fall, but the old man made it through the obstacle course of books to the front door. Beadlesberry extended his fragile bony hand. "Delighted, valiant dragon hunter, delighted. Your fame precedes you."

Gruen beamed and engulfed Beadlesberry's hand in a giant fist. Tyler waited to hear the bones cracking, but the old man didn't even wince. Gruen opened his hand and let go.

Then he announced loudly, "Of course. I am the most famous and successful dragon hunter in Balara, if not the world. In fact, perhaps in the entire universe."

Beadlesberry nodded vigorously. "And did you have a pleasant journey down from the North?"

"Boring. I am looking forward to hunting this terrible dragon of yours. Who has seen the beast?" Gruen asked, looking around. His eyes focused on Tyler and he beckoned him over.

Tyler gingerly stepped around the piles of books and looked up at the giant. "Uh, I'm just a visitor to Balalac, sir. You'd have to ask the Mayor."

Gruen turned back to Beadlesberry. "So, Mayor of Balalac, who has seen this dragon?"

Beadlesberry coughed softly. "Well, no one has actually seen the beast, but the signs all point to the possibility of a dragon."

Gruen nodded. "Explain."

They all sat down at the table. The chair groaned under Gruen's huge body. Beadlesberry proceeded to tell the tale of the boiling lake and the midnight earthquakes. Tyler joined in and told him how Ellaby's mother had disappeared. "Don't you think that is a strange coincidence?" Tyler asked.

Gruen had closed his huge eyes and softly snored. Tyler thought he had gone to sleep. Just as he was about say something, Gruen sat up and pounded his fist on the table. Books bounced to the floor.

"Excellent, excellent, all things point to the presence of a mighty dragon. Now we must determine the origin of the dragon."

Beadlesberry winked at Tyler. "So young warrior, tell Gruen the Great your theory."

Tyler looked at Gruen's enormous fist and took a deep breath. He let it out in a gush of words. "Um, we, my friend Zack and me, oh, and Ellaby, she's the daughter of Dunby the Keeper of the Spa, well, we think there is a wizard at Maidenspa who is controlling the dragon."

Beadlesberry beamed. "Is this not the clever idea of a brave warrior? Comes from a long line of valiant warriors. Why I recall his great grandfather, Thelloneous Trent solved the Mystery of the Ogre of Ogg."

Wait a minute. How could this Beadlesberry know Tyler had a great grandfather named Thelloneous Trent? He rolled his eyes. Dummy, the old man had been pretending the whole time. He knew exactly what was going on. Tyler gritted his teeth and glared at Beadlesberry, but the old man just clasped his hands and grinned.

Lying old windbag. He had this sudden urge to put his hands around his scrawny chicken neck and squeeze. Tyler wouldn't put it past him to have stolen the pendant himself and hidden it just so they would have to find the wizard. That raven that kept showing up, Tyler bet it was Beadlesberry's bird. Maybe it was Beadlesberry himself, who knows what kind of magic he could do. The old man probably spoke bird or whatever they called it around here. Wait until Zack hears this, Tyler thought, he'll freak.

Tyler dug his fingernails into his palms. No sense in losing it. He just hoped the old man wasn't going to lay it on too thick. Gruen peered at Tyler from under his bushy, overhanging brows. "Tell him the rest, Tyler Trent," Beadlesberry cackled. "Tell him your great plan to catch the wizard." Tyler sent Beadlesberry a nasty look, then turned to Gruen and described the plan.

The giant went into a trance again. Tyler was prepared this time and when the huge fist slammed the table, he didn't even jerk, well maybe just a tiny jerk. "I will meet with these brave friends of yours and of course the little woofen. I do, however, like the sound of this Drumthwack, Keeper of the Debt. He might just be the sort of person who likes to make things difficult for others, hence his work.

"Of course, Dismar, the apothecary, has knowledge of potions and spells. Then there is Calamar, who may very well be a wizard hiding behind chocolate covered raisins in his gingerbread shop. My, my, so many choices."

He stood up, nearly touching the ceiling beams. "We will go and see what your friends have unearthed."

Gruen followed Tyler out of the bookstore and down the street. Suddenly a voice roared, "GRUEN." They stopped and turned. Bramble was pounding down the street, bags of food bouncing from his arms. Windows shook and heads peeked fearfully from doors. Tyler jumped back as Gruen shouted, "BRAMBLE." Tyler ducked out of the way when the two giants crashed together in a bear hug. He could feel the ground tremble under his feet and they circled around pounding each other on the back. Finally they broke apart.

Bramble turned to Tyler and announced, "My cousin, Gruen, the mighty Dragon Hunter." He thrust the bags of food at Tyler, who sagged under their weight. Tyler wondered what could possibly be in them. They were only having pizza.

Bramble grabbed his cousin by his shoulders. "You are famous throughout Balara."

"Indeed, cousin, I am famous throughout the world, if not the universe," Gruen said.

Bramble grinned, his giant teeth gleaming. "Is he not magnificent?"

Tyler nodded. He thought Gruen bragged a lot. Who knows, maybe he was the most famous dragon hunter in the world. How many dragon hunters could there be anyway? Tyler took a chance and asked, "Um, Gruen, how many dragon hunters are there?"

Gruen puffed out his chest and said, "Only one, the mighty Gruen."

Exactly what Tyler had thought, but he just nodded and handed the bags back to Bramble. "We're meeting Zack and Ellaby at the crossroads."

Gruen opened his mouth to speak, but Tyler put his finger over his lips and shook his head. He hoped Gruen was smart enough to understand that he didn't want to talk in front of Bramble. He would tell Crumble and there would go their plans.

Gruen nodded and asked Bramble about his life at Maidenspa. Tyler left them behind, running to get there before the giants. He wanted to warn the others that Bramble was coming. Pottaby ran to meet him, barking and jumping at his ankles. Zack leaned against the signpost stuffing chocolate into his mouth. Ellaby jumped up from the large stone where she had been sitting.

Tyler could hear the giants' voices. "Listen, it turns out that Gruen the Dragon Hunter is Bramble's cousin. He came into the bookshop while I was telling Beadlesberry the story. By the way, he's been lying to us all the time. He probably stole the pendant himself to keep us here. I bet it was that raven."

Zack looked bewildered. "Gruen stole the pendant?"

"No, jerk, Beadlesberry. But I don't really know that for sure. Anyway Gruen and me, we were coming out of the bookstore when Bramble came running down the street. Like I said, they're cousins. So now we can't talk about anything, because of Bramble. Come on; let's go back to the Inn. We'll talk about it later."

"Yeah, after pizza," Zack said. "Pizza stimulates the brain to think. It's a good problem-solver food."

Gruen and Bramble had reached them, but they were so engrossed in catching up on all theyears, they paid no attention to anyone else. Tyler was happy to delay any discussion until later. Maybe Zack was right, everything was better after pizza. Except he was sure the cheese would be black like the milk. Black pizza. He wondered whatthe tomato sauce would look like. Well, whatever it looked like, it would definitely taste like pizza. At Maidenspa everything tasted just the way you expected it to taste.

He heard the beating of wings and looked up. Sure enough, the raven was perched on the tree branch staring down at him. Tyler stuck out his tongue. The bird ruffled his feathers and, plop, something landed on Tyler's head. "Yuck," he said, fingering the wet and sticky mess. "Thanks a lot."

The bird cawed and flapped his wings.

Chapter 15

Black Pizza and Magical Lanterns

Everyone sat down for dinner that night, even Bramble and Crumble. They feasted on 10ten huge black and gray pizza pies. Zack leaned over and whispered, "This is so gross, like mud pies." Tyler jabbed him in the ribs, but secretly he agreed. At least they tasted just like pizza. Bramble and Gruen ate three apiece. Tyler noticed that Ellaby just picked at one small piece.

His mouth still full, Gruen turned to Bramble and mumbled, "Wonderful, wonderful. I have never tasted anything like it in all my travels through Balara."

Bramble nodded at Crumble. "She is the master of the kitchen, Gruen. A wizard at the art of cooking."

Zack choked on his food and Tyler smacked him on the back, which only made him cough harder. No one seemed to notice.

Crumble beamed. "Thank Tyler Trent our fearless warrior. He gave me the secret recipe. What is it called again, Tyler?"

Tyler swallowed. "Um, pizza."

"Stupendous," Gruen said, stuffing another whole slice into his mouth. Ellaby winked at Tyler, who blushed.

After dinner, Gruen let out a huge belch and patted his stomach. "Now my friends I think I shall walk along the lake. Does someone wish to join me?" He glared at Tyler who jumped up almost overturning his chair. Zack and Ellaby stood up also.

Bramble shook his head. "We would like to walk with you Gruen, mighty dragon hunter, but I have to repair a leak in the roof before dark. All the shaking from our midnight earthquakes has loosened some of the tiles. Perhaps we will see you later."

Gruen nodded. "Ah, Bramble, you are much needed here at Maidenspa, that is good. I am proud of you cousin. You also married the best cook in Balara."

Bramble grinned at Crumble, who should have turned as red as the pizza sauce, but only went a darker gray. "Oh, go on, you flatterer. We will see you later tonight," she laughed.

Ellaby and the two young warriors followed the giant dragon hunter down to the lake. Pottaby ran alongside them. Gruen sat down beneath a tree and the others sat around him. Pottaby curled up in Ellaby's lap. Gruen said, "Now, tell me what you learned in town today. Ellaby, you begin the tale." Then he closed his eyes and appeared to fall asleep. Tyler looked at Zack and shrugged.

Ellaby didn't seem to notice and said, "I went to the apothecary to get herbs for Crumble's special tea. Dismar was in a foul mood today. It appears that one of his shelves of herbs fell over last night during the earthquake and all the herbs spilled out. They were all mixed together and he was unable to sort them. He had to throw away the whole mess. He spent the entire time grumbling about dragons and what a terrible situation this is. Soon he was almost in tears. Poor Esmara had to keep patting his back and telling him that it would be all right as soon as Gruen the dragon hunter arrived. I felt sorry for him, he was so distressed."

"Doesn't sound like a wizard to me," Zack said.

Tyler shrugged. "Me either."

"Unless he was pretending," Gruen said, never opening his eyes.

Ellaby shook her head. "I did not get that feeling. He seemed most sincere. I truly do not believe Dismar is the wizard. I have known him all my life and he is truly a gentle man."

Tyler turned to Zack. "What about Calamar?"

"Honest, Tyler, how can somebody who does nothing all day long but make and sell candy be a wizard. I mean, he's so cool."

Tyler rolled his eyes at Zack. "Listen, forget your stomach for a minute. What did he say?"

"Well, I went in and asked for a bag of chocolate mints." Zack's eyes glazed over.

Tyler shook him. "Oh man, Zack, forget the chocolate mints, will you? What happened then?"

Zack said, "Well I asked him what he thought was happening at Maidenspa and why the water was boiling every morning and the ground shook every night. So he said that there must be something under the ground making this happen, maybe like a dragon. Then I asked him if he knew how this dragon might have gotten under the ground and he said, "Magic."

"He did? He actually said the word magic?" Tyler was all excited.

"So what," Zack said. "It doesn't mean anything. Everybody knows it has to be some kind of magic. I mean, dragons don't just appear and disappear, at least I think they don't." He turned to Gruen. "Do they?"

Gruen shook his head. "It depends."

Tyler made a face. "That helps. Depends on what?" Gruen didn't answer. Tyler turned to Zack, spread his arms and shrugged. Gruen looked as though he had fallen asleep again. Tyler tilted his head and peered at the giant's face. He had the urge to poke him in the chest. Gruen suddenly sat up and Tyler bounced back, almost losing his balance.

"It depends on whether the dragon is real or something or someone under the spell of a wizard," Gruen said.

Zack lifted his eyebrows. "You mean there's more than one kind of dragon? Isn't a dragon just a dragon?"

Gruen looked at Zack like he was a bug. "Of course not foolish boy. There are many kinds of dragons. Why, just last month in Banolara City I captured a slimy-toed gulla dragon with two heads. Last year there was the double spiked-tail leaping dragon of Bunwalla. Of course, both of those were real dragons. I fear that this time we face a magical dragon of horrendous proportions, a very angry one at that."

Tyler and Zack glanced at each other. Zack opened his mouth but nothing came out. Then Tyler spoke so softly they could barely hear his question. "How do you know this is a magical dragon, mighty Gruen?"

Gruen puffed out his chest and grinned. "Simple, young warrior. This dragon only wreaks havoc at night. Therefore, it must be something else during the day."

Tyler looked at Zack and mouthed "wreaks havoc?" Zack shrugged. Tyler never got that dictionary at Beadlesberry's Rare Books. He nodded and mumbled, "Uh, sure, simple."

Gruen puffed out more and Tyler was sure his buttons would pop. "A true dragon would cause chaos and destruction all the time. Except of course when it sleeps and even then great mists rise from its nostrils, obscuring everything around it. Why I recall the Brimballa dragon of '79 burned twelve forests before I sent it to…"

Ellaby jumped to her feet dumping Pottaby in heap on the grass.

"Your stories are fascinating, mighty Gruen, but perhaps we should hear what Pottaby learned from Kittythwack. I feel very strongly that Drumthwack is thewizard."

Tyler shook his head. "I still think Calamar might be a wizard. He acted awfully strange the first time we went in there for candy."

"He was fine today," Zack said. "Besides, how could anyone think a candy man could be a wicked wizard?"

Tyler answered, "Remember Willie Wonka?"

"Huh?" Zack said. "That was a character in a book." Tyler stared at Zack, a smile playing around his mouth. Zack smacked his forehead. "Stupid, stupid, of course, a character in a book."

Ellaby looked from Tyler to Zack. "What are you two talking about? Who is this Willie Wonka?"

Tyler changed the subject. "Forget it, it's not important. Let's hear what Pottaby has to tell us."

Gruen had closed his eyes again, but now they flew open and he leaned forward. "This woofen has a story to tell?"

Ellaby started pacing back and forth. "Yes. Drumthwack has a purren, Kittythwack. Pottaby went to meet her today. At great personal risk, I may add." Ellaby related the story of Dellthwacky's nose. "He said if he ever got hold of Pottaby, he would turn him into a griswaller." A quivering Pottaby pushed his head under Zack's arm. Tyler wondered what kind of a creature a griswaller was to make Pottaby so scared.

"This is a vengeful, evil magician," Gruen announced. He reached out and patted Pottaby. "Do not fret, little woofen. No one is going to turn you into a slimy, malodorous griswaller as long as Gruen the Mighty is around." Gruen laughed and the tree shook so hard, leaves fell down on their heads.

Now at least Tyler knew a griswaller was smelly and slimy. Maybe it was better not to know any more. Pottaby pulled his head out and started to woof again. Ellaby translated. "According to the purren, Drumthwack is very angry with my father and me because of Dellthwacky's nose. It also seems that he was once in love with my mother and when she married my father, he stopped speaking to them." Ellaby stopped the story and said, "I never knew that." She stared into space.

Pottaby woofed. "Oh, I am sorry," Ellaby said, continuing the story. "Kittythwack says that Drumthwack goes somewhere every night through a tunnel underneath the house. She is afraid to follow him because she might get lost in the dark. Kittythwack is afraid of the dark. He returns just before midnight."

Tyler interrupted. "So he gets back to his house before the earthquake starts. I wonder where he goes."

Pottaby woofed and Ellaby said, "Kittythwack had no idea. She did say the tunnel was behind a door that vanished as soon as Drumthwack came back into the house."

"Aha, a magic doorway," Gruen said.

"There's a disappearing doorway in the Inn, you know, and a staircase too." Zack added. "I got lost in one my first night here. Oops." He glanced quickly at Ellaby, who just smiled. She must have known all along.

"Right," Tyler said. "Pottaby helped me find him. As soon as we got out the doorway disappeared.

Gruen leaned forward. "Ellaby, do you know where the staircase leads?"

"It goes down into a tunnel under the ground," she answered. "Do you think this might be the same tunnel?" Ellaby bounced on her tiny feet. "Perhaps we can go down into the tunnel tonight. We can hide and follow Drumthwack when he comes along."

Zack pursed his lips. "I don't know about this. What if everything disappears when we're down there? What if there is more than one tunnel and we get lost? What if we go into the one tunnel and Drumthwack is in another? What if he sees us? What if…?"

Gruen rose to his feet and towered over them. "Enough Zack Vander. You are a warrior. Be brave and strong. We shall prevail."

Zack stared down at his feet. Tyler felt sorry for Zack. Secretly he agreed with him, but now he would never say so, especially in front of Ellaby.

"So will we go tonight?" Ellaby asked excitedly.

Gruen looked around at everyone. One by one they nodded. "Good, it is decided. Of course it may be that I cannot fit in the tunnel. Then you three will go alone."

Zack rolled his eyes, but kept quiet. The screaming heavy metal rock band was back in Tyler's chest. Why didn't this feel good?

Ellaby tilted her head. "I wondered about that, Gruen. It has been many years since Pottaby and I roamed those tunnels. Papa said it was too dangerous."

Zack looked up. "Dangerous?"

"Well, I was only a little girl and Pottaby was just a woofeny. I am sure it is perfectly safe now that we are older. Besides, we will be together and you are both such brave warriors. Then of course, there is Gruen the mighty dragon hunter to protect us."

"If he fits in the tunnel," Zack muttered.

"Are you afraid, Zack Vander?" Ellaby asked. "We can go without you."

"Did I say I was scared?" Zack muttered.

Tyler wondered how much protection Gruen would be against a wizard. Maybe they would all be turned into slimy griswallers tonight. Way to go jerk. Keep thinking like this and you'll be too scared to crawl out of bed. "What if the staircase is still missing? How can we find it?" Tyler asked.

"Do not worry, it will appear when we are ready," Ellaby answered.

Gruen rose to his full height. He looked down on them and said, "It is decided then. We go tonight when the clock chimes ten."

Tyler wondered if Gruen would even fit inside the staircase. It was awfully narrow. Why worry; the doorway was probably invisible anyway. They would probably never get beyond the hall.

Gruen lay down on the grass. "I shall rest now. Perhaps we will be fortunate to witness the transformation of this dragon by the Wizard of Maidenspa. I am most excited by the prospect." He closed his eyes and immediately began to snore. The lowest leaves on the trees rustled with each breath he exhaled.

Tyler wondered what would happen if Gruen really got excited. He followed the others back toward the Inn, thinking of leftover pizza. What did a slimy griswaller eat?

The boys sneaked into the kitchen and found the remains of the pizza pie. With no way to heat it, Tyler stuffed a slice of cold pizza into his mouth and wondered why time seemed to move so slowly when you wanted it to move fast. Zack bit into his second piece just as Crumble came in through the back door. "Out, out," she howled. "Out of my kitchen."

Tyler grabbed another slice and ran out through the dining room, Zack at his heels. They plopped down on the front porch, laughing. "I thought we were done for," Zack gasped. Tyler nearly choked as he tried to laugh and swallow at the same time. The sun was dropping lower in the sky and the shadows were growing longer.

Tyler wondered if this was the last slice of pizza he would ever have. He wanted to be home in his own bed in New York listening to the sounds of car horns blasting and sirens screaming, not climbing down disappearing staircases and crawling through tunnels chasing after a wizard. What if Drumthwack wasn't the wizard after all? Maybe he had business in the tunnels that had nothing to do with the dragon. Then who could it be? Tyler was getting a headache from all this confusion. They sat in silence watching the sun sink below the horizon.

Zack turned to Tyler and whispered. "Maybe we should just let Gruen look for the dragon?"

Tyler shook his head. "He probably won't even fit in the stairway. Besides, we have to do this or we'll never get home."

Zack shrugged and pulled back. "Hey, we can just go to Beadlesberry and tell him we're too scared to do it and that we want to go home right now."

Tyler rolled his eyes and pulled harder on Zack's arm. "He's not going to let us go until we solve the problem. Don't you understand? This is what it's all about."

"What, what's all about?" Zack asked.

"Going into the story. We have to solve whatever the mystery or problem is in the story before we can go back," Tyler said impatiently.

Zack groaned, "Oh man, oh man. This is a bummer. I don't want to be turned into a griswadder."

"Griswaller, and that's not going to happen," Tyler said.

The porch shook and a deep voice boomed, "It is time, young warriors." They leaped to their feet and spun around. Why did everybody sneak up on you around here, Tyler thought. "Come on. We'll be fine," Tyler said, pulling on Zack's arm.

Zack shook him off. "You'd better be right. 'Cause I don't feel so good right now." Head down, he followed Tyler and Gruen into the house.

Ellaby and Pottaby were waiting in the second floor hallway, staring at the blank wall. "Oh good, no door," Zack turned back. As Tyler reached out to stop him, the door suddenly appeared in the wall. Zack froze.

Ellaby looked up at Gruen. "This is the disappearing doorway, mighty dragon hunter. Inside is a staircase that leads down to the tunnels."

Tyler opened the door and Pottaby ran down a few steps. He turned and waited, tongue hanging out. Gruen put his head in the door, then his shoulder and finally turned sideways. He backed out. "I will never be able to fit inside. You will have to go alone. I shall search for a way in from the outside. Just tell me which direction to follow."

Ellaby said something in woofen and Pottaby raced down the stairs. He returned shortly and woofed. "Pottaby says to go toward the lake." Gruen nodded and left them in the hallway facing the disappearing door. "Here," Ellaby said, handing each boy a black metal lantern.

They entered the staircase and started down.

The door closed behind them cutting off the light. The lanterns began to glow in the darkness, growing brighter as they descended the stairs. Tyler couldn't figure out where the light came from. He glanced at Zack, who shrugged. There was no flame and it didn't work like a flashlight, yet the staircase was bright like it was in full sunlight. Must be some kind of magic lantern. Why not, it went with the disappearing staircase and the vanishing door. He'd have to ask Ellaby later, if there was a later.

The stairs suddenly ended and they faced a dark, narrow tunnel. Ellaby turned to Tyler and nodded. Tyler drew in a deep breath and squeezed

her arm. He could hear Zack groan faintly behind him. Then he took another deep breath and stepped out into the tunnel behind Pottaby.

Chapter 16

The Dragon's Lair

Pottaby's nails tapped faintly on the stone floor of the tunnel. Otherwise it was deathly silent. They came to a fork. Another tunnel, pitch black, led off to the right. Pottaby sniffed at the opening and then turned away and continued straight ahead. "I hope he knows where he's going," Zack whispered.

Tyler nodded, wondering the same thing. What if that was the tunnel the Wizard was taking. If he wasn't here yet, he could come up behind them. This was not a good idea. He tapped Ellaby on the shoulder and whispered into her ear. She bent down and spoke softly to Pottaby. He gently woofed. "He says someone has already passed this way. He is ahead of us."

The word ambush flickered across his mind, but he didn't think Drumthwack knew they were in the tunnels. He hoped they wouldn't end the night as slimy griswallers or dragon food.

The tunnel grew wider and pointy rocks appeared here and there. Pottaby suddenly stopped and softly woofed at Ellaby. "He says we must turn off the lights and follow him in the dark. We are near a cave," she murmured.

"How do you turn these off?" Zack said softly. "I don't even know how they turned on?" As he said it, the lanterns winked off.

Tyler shivered. The tunnel was a blot of black ink. Icy fingers of fear tickled his spine. They crept silently, feeling the walls. The tunnel seemed to curve. Then it straightened and Tyler could see a faint light ahead. Pottaby's tiny form moved toward the light.

Suddenly, Pottaby turned and ran back toward them. He jumped at Ellaby and woofed softly. She pulled Zack and Tyler close and whispered, "Pottaby says there is a huge cave up ahead and two people are inside. There is a large rock formation at the entrance to the cave where we can hide. Come."

The boys followed Ellaby and they edged behind large pointed boulders and crouched. They could hear a man's voice and then a woman answer. It was far away and echoed. Tyler could barely make out the voices. He felt Ellaby stiffen next to him. "What is it?" he whispered. She didn't answer. Instead she rose until her eyes were just above the rocks. The boys looked at each other and then also peered into the cavern.

It was enormous. The walls were pearly white and glowed with phosphorescent crystals. Crystals hung from the ceiling and rose from the floor. A giant silver cage stood in the middle of the cavern floor, set over a winding stream of water that seemed to disappear under the stone walls of the cave. A tiny woman sat on a pillow on the floor of the cage. There was a mat beside her with several bowls and a spoon. A blanket lay on the stone floor beside her. She had long black hair and wore a robe. She seemed to be crying.

A man stood by the cage. He wore a long cloak that covered his entire body. There was even a hood that hid his face. It was impossible to tell who was under the cloak. "You will never leave here, my beautiful Doraby. You are mine forever." Then he roared with laughter. The hideous sound bounced across the cavern and echoed off the stone walls. The woman covered her ears and pulled the cloak tighter around her body. She huddled there shaking as he continued to laugh.

He stopped suddenly and leaned toward the cage. "In a short time you will become a dragon again, spouting fiery flames into the stream, boiling the lake at Maidenspa. The earth will shake with your rage and I will rejoice in everyone's misery."

Then he raised his arms, waving a silver wand, and bellowed, "I CALL UPON REVENGE, MALACAR. I CALL UPON TRANSMUTATION, LACARAM. I CALL UPON ALL MY POWERS. MAKE HAVOC IN THIS WORLD."

He laughed again and then said, "Goodnight my dearest Doraby." Tyler pulled the others down beneath the rocks as the Wizard strode swiftly toward the tunnel. He paused at the entrance to the cavern. Tyler could hear him breathing just on the other side of the boulder. Tyler's heart pounded so fast, he was sure the Wizard could hear it. Any second and they would be discovered.

"Little fools, think they can outwit the Wizard of Balalac. Nobody is as powerful as I." Then he cackled and moved away into the darkness of the tunnel.

Zack let out the breath he had been holding. "I'm gonna throw up," he said.

Tyler didn't feel too well himself. He turned to Ellaby, but she was gone. He jumped up and saw her running across the cavern toward the cage. Pottaby was chasing after her. Tyler ran. "Come back," he called. "He may not be gone." Ellaby paid no attention. Instead she knelt down beside the cage and reached in. "Mother."

The woman inside looked up and then jumped up and ran to the bars. She reached through and pulled Ellaby close. "Oh my dear sweet baby. I have been so worried about you. How is your father?"

"He has gone off to find you, Mother. We thought you were…I mean when you disappeared, we didn't know what to think."

"He caught me at the edge of the woods and put me in this cage. He cast a spell on me." Doraby said, tears dropping from her eyes. Pottaby licked her hand. "Hello, Pottaby. Have you been a good woofen?" Pottaby woofed and wagged his tail.

"Oh, Mother, do you become a dragon every night?" Ellaby said.

Doraby nodded as Tyler and Zack reached the cage. Doraby looked up at them. "Who are you?"

Ellaby answered, "These are Tyler Trent and Zack Vander, two young warriors. They have come to vanquish the wizard. Gruen the dragon hunter is also here to help. Mayor Beadlesberry sent for him."

Tyler said, "I'm sorry to meet you this way, but I'm glad you are alive. We'll help you. We just have to figure out who the Wizard is."

"Right, um Mrs.um Doraby," Zack said. "Can you tell us who the wizard is?"

"It's Drumthwack, right?" Ellaby said, squeezing her mother's hand.

Doraby clutched her throat. "Oh no. Hurry, you must run as fast as you can. I feel the fire beginning in my throat." She ran to the other side of the cage. A tiny tail was starting to grow out of her back. Her face was growing longer. "Get out of here, now. Run, Aaargh."

"Mother, noooooo." Ellaby screamed as Tyler grabbed her and pulled her toward the tunnel. Zack scooped up Pottaby and ran after them. They plunged through the darkness stumbling over the rocks. The lanterns suddenly glowed brighter and brighter. Just as they reached the staircase, the tunnel walls started to shake. They could hear a distant roar, as Doraby, now a dragon, pounded against the bars of her cage, shaking the earth.

Tyler dragged a crying Ellaby up the stairs, praying that the door would be there. He could hear Zack pounding behind him. The wall was solid. Tyler pounded against the wall. Pottaby woofed and the door suddenly appeared and Tyler flung it open. They all piled into the hallway and fell in a heap on the floor. Pottaby wriggled out of Zack's arms, woofing. The wall was solid again, but everything else was shaking. "Come on," Zack cried. "We have to get downstairs."

They raced down the stairs and into the dining room. Gruen was frantically pacing back and forth. Crumble and Bramble huddled under the table. Ellaby pulled away from Tyler and collapsed in tears in Crumble's arms.

Gruen looked at Tyler and Zack, who nodded. Then he walked away from the others and waved them over. "You saw the wizard and the dragon?"

Tyler nodded and told him the story. "We still don't know who the Wizard is. There wasn't time for Doraby to tell us."

"And we never saw his face," Zack added.

Gruen frowned. "Such a cruel and wicked spell, to take a loving mother and helpmate from her family and turn her into a dragon. This is a most evil Wizard."

"We did hear his spell, or something that sounded like a spell," Zack said.

"Right," Tyler said. "He was calling on these powers and saying strange words."

"Do you remember the words," Gruen asked.

Tyler shrugged and looked at Zack, who shook his head. "We'll have to think about it. I never heard them before."

Zack said, "They sounded familiar, almost like they were the same words, but different some how. He also had this silver wand he kept waving around."

"I didn't see any wand. Maybe Ellaby remembers," Tyler suggested.

They all turned to Ellaby, but she was curled up in a ball on the ground. Crumble was patting her back. "I think we'd better forget it tonight," Zack said.

Ellaby stirred and turned a tear-stained face toward them. "Please, help my mother. She does not deserve to suffer in this way. This is a monstrous thing the Wizard has done."

Crumble dripped tears. "You are so strong, young warrior. I know you and Zack will prevail in this battle with the Wizard."

"Yes, yes, with help of my cousin Gruen, the mighty dragon hunter," Bramble said.

Ellaby stood and looked up at Gruen, her wet eyes pleading. Gruen kneeled down and placed his enormous hand on her tiny shoulder. "I, Gruen, the most powerful dragon hunter in Balara, if not the universe, promise that Doraby, the lovely, will be freed from this terrible spell and the vile and venomous Wizard of Maidenspa will be thwarted."

Here we go again, Tyler thought.

The shaking finally stopped and they all trooped upstairs to their rooms. Tyler threw off his clothes and snuggled under soft warm covers. How were they going to beat the Wizard, when they still didn't know who he was? Tyler fell asleep trying to remember the words the Wizard used in the cavern.

Pottaby padded in and stood up against the bed looking at Tyler. Then he went across the hall and checked on Zack. Satisfied, he settled down in the hallway between their rooms, put his head on his paws and went to sleep, snuffling softly.

Tyler dreamed. He was running down the middle of Park Avenue chased by an enormous purple and green striped dragon. He could feel the heat of the dragon's fiery breath on his back. At the corner of 52nd Street, his feet left the ground and he soared into the sky, above the tall buildings. He looked down at the dragon, who was bellowing with rage. Showers of sparks bounced off the stone and brick buildings. Tyler laughed and laughed, flying just out of range of the dragons whipping tail and flaming nostrils. At 54th Street he plummeted to earth. He could feel hot dragon's breath on his face as he plunged toward the orange flames shooting out of the dragon's mouth. In a moment he would be roasted like a marshmallow. In the distance he could see Gruen, the dragon hunter, barreling down the street toward the dragon, waving a giant silver wand. Somehow, he knew Gruen would never make it in time. "Ramalac," he shouted from six feet above the dragon. The dragon disappeared.

Tyler opened his eyes, drenched in sweat. "Ramalac," he mumbled and drifted back to sleep until the sun streamed across his eyes and the woodpecker began his morning tattoo on the tree outside his window.

Chapter 17

The Wizard of Balalac

"Wake up, wake up."

Tyler opened his eyes and squinted against the light. He turned his head away from the window and stared into Ellaby's face, not two inches from his own. Tyler pulled the blanket up over his body. He was only wearing his briefs. Ellaby continued to shake him. "Wake up, Tyler Trent."

"Hey, what's all the noise," Zack said, yawning in the doorway.

Ellaby stood up, hands on hips. "I know who the wizard is."

Tyler sat up hugging the blanket to his chest. "You do?"

Zack jumped on the bed followed by Pottaby. "So who is it?" he asked, excitedly.

"It is Calamar," Ellaby exclaimed.

"The candy man?" Zack said, shaking his head.

Tyler dismissed Zack's words. He was thinking with his stomach again. "How do you know?"

She plopped down on the edge of the bed. Tyler edged away toward the other side. "I talked to Crumble last night after the earthquake. She told me that it was Calamar who wanted to marry my mother, not Drumthwack. She said he never married because he has been in love with my mother all this time. He hates my father." Tears floated over her eyelids. She sniffed. "I think he is doing this just to get back at my father."

Zack suddenly stiffened."Listen, you know those magic words the wizard was shouting last night. I just remembered one of them, malacar."

There was silence. Then Tyler smacked his fist against his head. "Of course," Tyler said. "An anagram."

Ellaby wrinkled her forehead. "A what?"

Zack said, "An anagram. It's a play on letters. You take one word and make others by moving around the letters. You know, like, Calamar, malacar."

Ellaby nodded. "Of course, the other word was lacaram."

"So he must use anagrams of his name to cast spells," Tyler said.

Zack jumped off the bed and began pacing. "Lacaram, lacaram. That was havoc. He used that to created havoc on the world."

"Right," Tyler said, almost dropping the blanket. "Malacar was transmutation." Tyler turned to Ellaby. "That's how he turns your mother into a dragon every night."

"That must mean it isn't permanent. I bet he has to go into the cave and cast the spell each time," Zack said.

"So how do we stop him?" Ellaby asked, brushing the tears from her cheeks.

"We use his own words against him," Zack said.

"What if they only work if he says them?" she asked.

Tyler turned to Zack. "She's right. It might not work if we use the words because we're not wizards. We have to stop him from going through the tunnels into the cave."

Zack rolled his eyes. "He's a wizard, remember? What's to stop him from turning us all into griswallers, whatever they are? He can probably cast a spell to stop our spell, if it even worked."

"It was Drumthwack who said griswallers, remember? Let me think, but first let me get dressed," Tyler said.

"Oh, sorry," Ellaby said, jumping off the bed. "I'll just wait downstairs." She hurried out of the room, Pottaby's tiny paws clicking after her.

Tyler went into the bathroom and washed. He pulled on his jeans and tee shirt. Then he ran wet fingers through his hair trying to flatten the curls that stood up. Shaking his head at the image in the mirror, he went down the hall toward the stairs. The door to the tunnels was back, but Tyler hardly glanced at it. Zack was sitting on the top step waiting. Tyler sat down next to him. "I don't know what we're going to do, Zack. I mean, we're not warriors."

Zack shrugged, "Don't look at me. I don't know the first thing about fighting wizards."

"Do you think maybe Beadlesberry has some ideas or maybe a book on fighting wizards?" Tyler suggested. "I mean, he's probably a wizard himself."

"You know, sometimes you come up with good ideas, Tyler. And sometimes, you come up with lousy ideas, like disappearing bookstores."

Tyler made a face at Zack. "Hey man, how could I to know we

would end up stuck here fighting wizards?"

Zack looked down at his shoes. "I bet there's a national manhunt for us now. We're probably on milk cartons all over the country. I bet they had a special assembly in school all about us."

Tyler put his arm around Zack's shoulder. "I'm sorry, Zack. I'm really sorry."

Zack shrugged off the arm and stood up. "Forget it, we're stuck here at least until we solve the problem, so let's think about how to do that."

Tyler watched his friend walk slowly down the stairs. He felt sick to his stomach. His throat was closing and he could feel tears parked behind his eyes, just waiting to shift into gear and spill out. Tyler took a deep breath and shook his head. He had to keep a cool head. There was enough time to be a baby if and when he was home in his own bed. Then he could crawl under the covers and bawl. Of course, if he were in his own bed, he wouldn't have any reason to cry. Why was everything so complicated? Tyler reached for the bannister and pulled himself up. He felt like an old man, older even than Beadlesberry, who was immortal. Tyler followed Zack downstairs.

The dining room was silent during breakfast. Everyone picked at the lumpers and zoggs. Pottaby curled up under Zack's chair. Crumble glared at the woofen and then went silently back to the kitchen. Even Gruen only ate two servings. Finally, Tyler couldn't stand it anymore. He pushed back his chair and announced, "What if we stole Calamar's wand?"

Zack turned a shade of green that Tyler had never seen before. "You mean break into his store?"

Tyler shrugged. "It's not such a terrible plan. You could pretend you want to buy some candy and distract him. I could try to get in through the back of the store."

"How do you even know he keeps the wand there? We're not even sure it's Calamar." Zack was breathing fast. "What if he hears you? He'll turn me into a griswaller or something worse."

"You worry too much, Zack Vander," Ellaby said. "I will accompany you and help to distract Calamar."

Tyler said, "So, Zack, you coming?"

Zack looked around at all the faces staring at him. Even Pottaby sat in the doorway wagging his tail. Zack rolled his eyes and nodded. Tyler grinned and slapped his friend on the back.

Gruen rose. "I will follow the tunnels again above the ground and try to find the cavern. Perhaps there is another entrance. If we can rescue the lovely Doraby before the evil Wizard returns tonight, then we can thwart his wicked spell."

"We couldn't find a door to the cage, Gruen," Zack said.

Gruen nodded. "A magic cage for a magical dragon. We will have to reverse the spell somehow."

"It's probably one of the anagrams of his name," Tyler said.

"Anagrams?" Guren and Crumble asked at the same time. Ellaby explained their theory about Calamar's magic words.

Crumble nodded. "While you are away, I shall write down as many of these anagrams as possible. Please be very careful, my dear sweet child. You too, mighty warriors. Pizza for everyone when you return."

Zack perked up. "Maybe you could put some pepperoni on top of the pizza this time?" Crumble wrinkled her brow and looked at Ellaby, who shrugged.

Tyler grabbed Zack's arm. "Use your brain, Zack. They don't have pepperoni in Balalac," he whispered.

"Uh, right, sorry, Crumble. Forget it, your pizza is perfect just the way it is," Zack said quickly, edging out of the room.

When they reached the bottom of the porch steps, Gruen turned toward the lake and the others followed the road to town. Gruen turned back for a moment and said in a booming voice, "Be very careful, my friends. Do not incur the fury of this vile wizard."

Tyler nodded and looked at Zack, who had a smirk on his face. Ellaby seemed to understand just what Gruen was saying. Pottaby danced ahead of them as they approached the overhanging trees. Tyler caught the flicker of black feathers through the leaves. The raven was still following them.

The closer they got to town, the harder Tyler's heart pounded. Zack had begun to lag behind after the crossroad sign. Now he was a good 20 feet behind them. Ellaby moved quickly, head up and arms swinging, but Tyler could see her lips pressed tightly together. At the edge of town, Tyler and Ellaby stopped and waited for Zack to catch up. "Okay," Tyler said. "So we each know what to do?"

Zack barely nodded. Ellaby said, "Are you sure you do not want me to go with you, Tyler Trent?"

"You go with Zack; I'll take Pottaby," Tyler said.

"You do not speak woofen, Tyler Trent," Ellaby pointed out.

"We'll manage. It's more important to keep Calamar busy out front."

Ellaby gritted her teeth. "I just hope I can keep from leaping on the counter and pounding his face."

Tyler put his hand over his mouth to hide his smile. He could just picture tiny Ellaby giving Calamar a bloody nose. "I thought that was Pottaby's job, you know, breaking people's noses?"

Ellaby tried not to smile, but couldn't stop herself. Even Zack laughed. Tyler felt better already. His heart had slowed. He could hear his father's voice, "Laughter makes everything seem better, Tyler." So he laughed too.

They separated. Zack and Ellaby continued down the main street and Tyler and Pottaby went behind the buildings along the grass. He had to be very careful not to be seen by Dismar or his family when he passed behind the apothecary.

There was nobody in the yard and the door was closed. Tyler moved quickly past the store. The bookshop was invisible, but the Raven sat on the fence preening its feathers. Tyler resisted throwing a stick at the big black bird. He was tired of Beadlesberry's stupid games.

There was the confectionery. Tyler carefully openedthe gate that led into the back yard. Pottaby stayed close to his legs. The gate squeeked and Tyler froze, holding his breath. Now his head was pounding. Nothing happened and he let out his breath in a whoosh. He hoped Zack and Ellaby were already inside keeping Calamar busy. He tiptoed to the door and turned the knob. The door was locked.

Stupid, stupid, why did he think it would be unlocked? Tyler turned to the window. It was open a few inches. He pushed up and the window rose slowly. Tyler stuck his head in the window and looked around. There was a bucket below the window. He swung a leg over the sill and carefully stepped down next to the bucket. Then he pulled his body in and brought his other leg over. He reached outside and lifted Pottaby up and through the window.

He heard the sound of the doorbell and Zack's voice faintly mingled with the sound of the door closing. Okay, they were in; now for the wand. Where would a wizard keep his wand? Tyler walked silently around the room. There was so much stuff. Shelves and shelves of books, pans, ladles, molds. There were at lease three closets. He would never find the wand. It might not even be here. Maybe Calamar took it home with him every night. Wherever home was. Tyler pushed those thoughts out of his head. It had to be here, nothing else was acceptable.

He carefully opened the first closet. Boxes and bins of chocolate.

He opened the second closet. Bags of flour and sugar. Finally, Tyler opened the third closet. There was the purple cloak. At least they knew now that Calamar was the Wizard. Tyler couldn't see anything else in the closet. Suddenly, Pottaby pushed past him. He stood up against the far wall and a panel of wood moved to the right.

Pottaby sat down and wagged his tail. "Good boy," Tyler whispered, patting his head. The woofen had a special knack for finding invisible doors and hidden panels. Tyler leaned down and reached into the opening. He felt around and pulled out a long, thin wooden box covered with strange carvings. There was a tiny lock. Pottaby's key.

Tyler pushed his hand deep in his pocket and fished out the key. It fit perfectly. He turned the key and lifted the lid. There was the silver wand. Tyler shut the box and slipped it into his jacket pocket with the key. He carefully closed the panel door and turned around. Just as he was about to step out of the closet he heard Zack's voice raised almost to shouting. "Wait, Calamar, I don't have to have jelly beans, licorice is okay."

Tyler heard Calamar's voice just outside the door to the shop. "Nonsense, dear boy, I pride myself on meeting all my customer's needs. Just take a minute." As the door opened, Tyler grabbed Pottaby and shut them both in the closet. The window. He had left the window open. What if Calamar noticed? Tyler was sure Calamar could hear the blood pounding through his body like a waterfall. He tried not to breathe. Oh God, now he had to pee.

"Where is that jar of jelly beans?" Calamar muttered. Tyler heard the squeek of the closet doorknob as it slowly turned. That was it. His life was over. In ten seconds he would either be dead or turned into some hideous, smelly creature. Just as the door started to open, Calamar announced, "Aha, there you are." He slammed the door shut and Tyler heard his footsteps move away from the closet. Then the door to the shop closed and he heard Calamar say from far away, "Here, you are young Zack, jelly beans. Calamar always comes through."

Tyler's breath flew out of his mouth with a woosh. He pushed at the door to the closet but it was stuck. Tyler put down Pottaby and used both hands to feel for a handle.

There wasn't any doorknob in the inside. He tried again to push open the door, even leaned against it with his shoulder. A sliver of light penetrated through the edge of the door, but it wouldn't open. Tyler closed his eyes and fought down nausea. He was locked in the wizard's closet.

Then he felt Pottaby's paws against his leg. He bent down and lifted the little woofen. Pottaby softly woofed in his ear. “I don’t understand you,” Tyler whispered. He could feel tears behind his eyes. Pottaby woofed again and squirmed up on Tyler’s shoulder. Pottaby scratched at the back panel of the closet with his paw. Tyler turned around and pushed at the wall. It slid open with a soft click. Tyler could see nothing but a black hole.

Pottaby wriggled and Tyler put him down. Pottaby woofed softly and started forward. Tyler carefully felt along the stone wall. He could touch both sides of the passage, so he knew he was in a tunnel. He took a step forward and then another. He hoped he wasn't going to plunge down a flight of stairs. Instead, the floor sloped gently downward. Tyler’s hand brushed something metal. It was a lantern, just like the ones they had used to explore the tunnel from the Inn. Tyler pulled it down and it immediately radiated a beam of light. The panel snicked closed behind him. He had no choice now but to follow Pottaby through the tunnel.

They hadn’t gone far, when Pottaby stopped and stood up against a wooden panel in the stone wall. Tyler pushed at the panel and it silently opened. His heart pounding, Tyler put the lantern down and stepped through the doorway.

The room was huge and filled ceiling to floor with drawers. There was a large wooden table with one chair in the middle of the room. He walked slowly around. Each drawer had someone’s name printed on the outside. There was even a drawer marked Tyler Trent and another marked Zachery Vander. He pulled open the one with his name and inside was a piece of paper with a list, ten chocolate turtles – Calamar, three nights at Maidenspa Inn – Dunby. Of course, he was in Drumthwack’s room where he kept the record of debts. This was why Kittythwack had reported seeing Drumthwack going into the tunnels. His secret treasury was here. Tyler closed the drawer and looked around. “There has to be another way out of here, Pottaby. I don’t want to back into the tunnels again.”

Just then Tyler heard a sound from the other side of the room. A panel slid open near the floor and a large cat sauntered slowly through the opening. Pottaby ran to meet her and they rubbed faces, softly woofing and purring. Tyler grinned. This had to be Kittythwack, the purren. She was beautiful with long thick, curly hair and bright eyes. Tyler had never seen a curly cat. Her tail waved like a flag in the wind. Pottaby turned and woofed, then followed Kittythwack to the opening in the wall.

Tyler got down on the floor and tried to wiggle after them. It was hard getting his shoulders through and he had to take off his jacket and push it through first. Then he scrunched his arms tightly against his side and twisted. He finally popped through, his shoulders scraped through his shirt.

He could feel fresh air against his face and lay there for a minute breathing deeply. Pottaby slurped his tongue across Tyler's face and woofed. "Okay, okay, give me a minute. It was hard getting through the doorway, I'm bigger than you." Tyler sat up and looked around. He was sitting in the grass outside a wooden building. "Thanks Kittythwack." Tyler reached over and stroked the purren.

Suddenly she stiffened and purred loudly. Pottaby woofed and pulled on Tyler's jeans. He sensed the danger even though he couldn't understand the language. "Is Drumthwack coming?" he asked. Pottaby let go of Tyler's jeans and woofed again. Then he turned and raced off around the corner of the next building. Kittythwack climbed onto Tyler's lap and purred loudly.

A blond girl appeared at the corner of the building. She was wearing a flowered blouse and skirt. She quickly brought her hand up to cover her nose. This had to be Dellthwacky. "Oh, you are the brave warrior who has come to fight the dragon. I see you found my purren," she said through her hand.

"Um, yeah. She's beautiful," Tyler said.

"Curly purrens are very rare," she mumbled.

"I'm sorry. I didn't understand you. Why are covering your face?" Tyler asked innocently.

She said louder, "I had an accident. Hurt my nose."

"Let's see," Tyler said, standing up suddenly.

She jumped back and grabbed the wall to keep her balance. Her nose was a little red and swollen, but not terrible. Tyler smiled. "You have a nice nose. You should stop covering it."

She stepped forward again and didn't cover her nose. "Do you really think so?" she asked.

"Sure. I've seen lots of noses, and yours is, um, as nice as any I've seen." Oh man, Tyler thought, this is sick.

Dellthwacky came even closer and smiled. "My name is Dellthwacky, but you can call me Dell. Do you have a girlfriend?"

"Uh, sort of," Tyler said.

"Oh," she said softly, looking down at the ground. "Is she pretty?"

Tyler shrugged. "Listen, I gotta go. Nice talking to you. Um, don't worry about your nose. It's fine."

Dellthwacky lifted her face and smiled. Two dimples appeared in her cheeks. The sun glinted off her light curls. Tyler gulped. Then she lowered her eyes and said softly, "Thank you brave warrior. I hope you find the wizard and slay the dragon."

Tyler tried to say something, but nothing came out of his mouth, so he nodded, then turned and ran. Pottaby was waiting for him around the corner. Tyler leaned against the side of the building and closed his eyes. Talking to girls was getting more and more complicated.

He pushed off the wall and raced as fast as he could to the crossroads, Pottaby panting along behind him. Tyler fell on the grass under a tree, feeling the wet licks of Pottaby's tongue on his face. He hugged the woofen and tried to slow the pounding in his heart and head. Maybe he would skip girls altogether and go back to his video games and books.

The box cut into his side, so he eased it out of his pocket. Tyler wondered what the carvings meant. Maybe Gruen could help. He felt a splat of wet hit his hand and looked up. The Raven sat on a branch overhead moving its head forward and back, back and forward. The dumb bird had peed on him again, and now he was laughing.

Tyler jumped up and yelled, "I know you Beadlesberry; you can't hide. I know you took the pendant. You think this is funny, don't you." The Raven opened its beak and squawked loudly.

"Who are you screaming at, Tyler Trent?"

Tyler spun around. Ellaby and Zack were standing in the road staring at him. He must have looked like a lunatic. He pointed to the tree. "The stupid Raven was back again and he peed on my hand. Then he sat there laughing at me." Tyler swiped his hand across his jeans. Yuck.

Ellaby looked up at the tree. "There is nothing in the tree, Tyler Trent."

Tyler looked up. She was right. The tree was empty. He looked at Zack. Surely he would understand, but Zack was busy stuffing a piece of chocolate in his mouth. Tyler grabbed the bag of candy and shook a large chocolate turtle into his hand. He bit down and sighed.

At least the chocolate tasted the same, even though it was black instead of brown. The world might end, but chocolate was still chocolate. He handed the bag back to Zack.

"Did you get it?" Zack asked.

Tyler grinned and nodded. Then he pulled out the box and opened it. The silver wand shone in the sunlight. Ellaby shivered. She reached out and touched the wand. "Poor Mama," she said sadly.

"We'll save her, Ellaby, don't you worry." Tyler sounded a lot more confident than he felt. He looked at Zack. "Did he suspect anything?"

Zack shook his head. "We kept him too busy finding candy. Ellaby kept changing her mind about what she wanted and how much she wanted. Did you have any trouble?"

Tyler said, "The door was locked, but I climbed in a window. There was so much junk back there. I never would have found it if Pottaby hadn't opened this secret panel in the back of one of the closets."

"I was a wreck when Calamar went back for the jelly beans," Zack said.

"We were so scared he would find you." Ellaby bent down and stroked the woofen, whispering in his ear. Pottaby wagged his tail and softly woofed.

Tyler told them what happened and how Pottaby found the entrance to the tunnel. He finished with the story of Dellthwacky's nose. Zack laughed. "Man, I wish I could have been there."

"It wasn't a bbig ddeal," Tyler said.

"So why are you stammering?" Zack asked.

"Just shut up, jerk," Tyler growled.

"I do not understand. You were very kind to Dell, Tyler Trent. You should be very proud of yourself," Ellaby said.

Tyler looked at Ellaby. Maybe he wouldn't give up girls after all. Zack punched his arm. Tyler turned, but Zack danced away. "Now what?" Tyler asked.

"What if we blocked the entrance to the tunnel? Then he would not be able to get to the cavern at all," Ellaby suggested.

"That might work," Tyler said. "How?"

Zack shrugged. "You're the chief wizard chaser."

Tyler frowned at Zack. "No I'm not. We're all in this together. You want to save Doraby as much as we do."

"We will use rocks and build a wall," Ellaby said. "Come along, brave warriors, we have work to do."

Tyler grinned at Zack and tapped his head. Quickly, they followed Ellaby toward the Inn at Maidenspa.

Chapter 18

Thwart the Wizard

Gruen was pacing back and forth in front of the porch when the three conspirators returned to the Inn. He lumbered down the path to meet them, gesturing wildly. "I found it, I found it."

"Found what?" Tyler asked.

"The other entrance to the cave. It is just beyond the woods on the other side of the lake."

"That is truly wonderful, Gruen," Ellaby said, smiling for the first time in days. "Now you will be able to help us free Mama."

Gruen puffed out his chest. Tyler thought he might start pounding it with his fists like a gorilla, but Gruen just strutted down the path in front of them. "We have the wand, Gruen," Tyler said to his back.

Gruen spun around. "Excellent, excellent. I knew you were fierce warriors. You have done well, Tyler Trent, and you, Zack Vander."

They reached the steps to the porch and sat down. "Now what?" Zack asked.

Crumble came out of the Inn and placed her hand on Ellaby's head. She gently stroked her hair and Ellaby leaned back against her legs. "You have returned unharmed. I was truly worried. Did you find the wand?"

Tyler held up the small box and Crumble nodded. "Good. I have deciphered a number of those words you call anagrams. I have written 16 different variations of Calamar, then I had stop to prepare the pizza." She pulled a long sheet of paper out of her pocket and began to recite, "macalar, maralac, laracam, lamarac, lamacar, ralamac, racalam, ramacal, amracal, armacal, acamal, caralam, camalar, cramala…"

As soon as she paused to breathe, Tyler jumped in, "Too many. We'll never find the right word and besides, who knows if it will even work for us."

Zack mumbled, "We should hold the wand for ransom."

Tyler leaped up, "What did you say?"

Zack looked up and said in a louder voice, "I said, we should hold the wand for ransom."

Tyler slapped his friend on the back. "Sometimes you come up with brilliant ideas, Zack." Tyler turned to the rest of the group, but he could see their bewildered expressions. "Ransom, you know, when you take something or someone and ask for something back in return."

Ellaby's smiled and her face glowed. "Of course, we offer Calamar the wand in exchange for Mama."

"There is but one problem," Gruen said. "What will prevent him from turning everyone into gorabungs or worse as soon as he has the wand back in his possession."

Zack looked at Gruen, "Gorabungs? Are they worse than griswallers?"

"Much worse," Gruen said gravely. "They have huge fangs and drool."

Zack hugged himself. "Great," he muttered.

"Come inside and eat pizza while it is hot. You think better when the stomach is full and happy." Crumble said, taking Ellaby's hand and leading her into the house.

"Great idea," Zack said. "I'm right behind you." One by one, the others followed. Tyler trailed behind. There had to be a way to keep Calamar from taking revenge on them all.

They ate in silence. Suddenly Zack shouted, "I've got it."

"What?" Tyler shouted, choking on a mouthful of pizza.

"Please stop shouting," Ellaby said. "We can all hear you perfectly, Tyler and Zack.

"I'm sorry," Zack said, "I was excited. We'll confront him in front of the whole town. He can't turn everybody into slimy creatures, right?"

"Excellent plan, young warrior," Gruen announced.

"Sure, we get Beadlesberry to call a town meeting and then we tell everybody what Calamar did and we show them his wand," Zack said.

"Hey, it just might work," Tyler agreed.

"I think it is a wonderful idea, Zack Vander." Ellaby smiled.

Zack's face flushed as red as his hair. "Uh, thanks, Ellaby."

Tyler rolled his eyes. "Okay, so somehow we have to free Doraby tonight before Calamar the Wizard turns her into a dragon again."

Zack continued, "Then we get Beadlesberry to call a town meeting tomorrow morning right here at the lake."

"And we produce Mama and the wand," Ellaby said.

"And expose this Calamar for the treacherous, vile creature that he is," Gruen finished.

All heads turned at the sound of clapping from the kitchen doorway. Crumble beamed at them. "This calls for putty for dessert."

After lunch, Ellaby volunteered to go into town and find Beadlesberry. The others set off to free Doraby from her prison.

Zack stopped and stared at the solid wall facing them. "Now what? The doorway is gone."

Tyler felt along the wall, but there was nothing. "Great, we'll have to find another way inside."

"Where's Pottaby?" Zack asked. "He'll be able to make the door appear."

Tyler shrugged, "I think he went with Gruen."

Zack slid down on the floor and leaned back against the wall. "Get up, Zack. I have an idea. You'll have to pretend something, though," Tyler said.

Zack wrinkled his brow and frowned. Tyler leaned down and whispered in his ear. Zack grinned and jumped up. "Okay. You're sure she's pretty."

"Beautiful," Tyler said.

"She better be, or you're dead," Zack said, bouncing down the stairs.

Half an hour later, Tyler tapped on the door to Drumthwack's house. The door opened a crack and Tyler could just see yellow curls and one eye peer around the edge of the door. Then the door flew open and Dellthwacky stood there, her dimples in all their glory. Kittythwack wound herself around Tyler's legs. He could hear Zack take a breath. "Um, Dell, I wanted you to meet my friend, Zack Vander."

Dell sighed. "You must be the other brave warrior. I am so honored to meet you Zack Vander. Please call me Dell."

"Nice to meet you, too," Zack said. Then he turned to Tyler. "You and Ellaby were right. She is beautiful."

Dell blushed and covered her mouth. "Ellaby said I was beautiful?"

Zack nodded. "Sure. In fact, she feels so bad about the accident she was crying. She said you were her best friend and she misses you."

Dell narrowed her eyes and stared at Zack. "Are you sure she said that? I thought Lisamara was her best friend."

Zack shook his head. "I'm sure she said you were." He looked at

Tyler who nodded, scratching a sudden itch on his upper lip. Zack's fingers were crossed behind his back.

Kittythwack stood up against Tyler's leg and extended her claws. "Ouch," Tyler said, pulling back his leg. Kittythwack purred and pranced back into the house, tail waving.

Dell said, "Naughty purren. I am so sorry. Kittythwack is usually very gentle."

Tyler rubbed his leg. "Dell, do you think you could get us back into the tunnel again?"

"You have found the wizard," she exclaimed.

Zack nodded. "It has to be a secret, though; you can't tell anybody."

She leaned forward. "I can keep a secret."

Zack and Tyler looked at each other. "I don't know," Tyler said.

"It might be very dangerous," Zack said.

Dell put her hands on her hips. "If you want my help, then you have to tell me."

The boys shrugged and told her the whole story. Dell's hand flew up to her mouth. "I cannot believe it is Calamar. He is so nice and he is the confectioner. Oh my, this is terrible. Poor Ellaby, she must be terrified for her mother. Imagine turning into a dragon every night."

"Remember, it's a secret. You can't tell anyone," Zack said.

"Oh, please do not worry. I would never tell. They can torture me and I will not tell," Dell said seriously.

Tyler grinned. "I don't think anybody's going to torture you, Dell. But we do need your help to get into the tunnel and block the entrance to the cave."

They followed Dellthwacky into the house. She led them to a wall in the entrance hall. She pressed against the panel and it opened to darkness. "Why does your father use the tunnels?"

Dell said, "He has a vault where he keeps important documents. He keeps it away from the house in case of a fire. Did you think my father was the wizard?"

Tyler shrugged, "Just for a little while. We were looking at anyone who used the tunnels."

"Besides, he did threaten to turn Pottaby into a griswaller," Zack said.

Dell laughed, "My father is a very kind man; he was just upset. He could no sooner turn a woofen into a griswaller than you could."

"Poor Pottaby," Tyler said, grinning. "He's petrified of your father."

"Pottaby was never in any danger. I shall speak to my father and Ellaby." Dell pushed at the panel in the wall and they were in the tunnels. "How do you propose to block the tunnel, Tyler and Zack?"

The boys looked at each other. "We're going to do it at the other end. There are lots of loose rocks and boulders. Gruen found another entrance to the cave. He and Bramble will meet us there and we'll close off the tunnel to the cave where he has Doraby. We just have to make sure the tunnels are clear so nobody gets trapped."

"Excellent plan. I shall come with you and assist," Dell said, marching ahead of them, Kittythwack at her side.

Tyler ran after her and pulled her to a stop. "Wait, we need you to get Ellaby and take her into the tunnels."

"Where is she?" Dell asked.

"She went to find Beadlesberry," Zack said.

Dell tossed her head. "This is becoming most complicated, brave warriors. However, I shall do my part." Tyler watched her until she disappeared behind the panel, and then they headed toward the cavern.

The tunnels were empty and dark. Finally they saw a light ahead and reached the entrance to the cavern. Bramble sat on the floor next to the cage patting Doraby's hand and talking softly. Pottaby sat in her lap. Gruen walked slowly around the cage testing each bar. They all looked up when the boys entered the cave.

"Ah, brave warriors, I have had no success in finding an opening to this cage. I fear it is a magical creation of the terrible Wizard of Maidenspa," Gruen said, tearing at his hair. Doraby caught her breath and trembled in her corner. Tears rolled down her cheeks. Bramble patted her hand harder.

"There has to be an opening somewhere," Tyler said. "We'll help you, Gruen." The warriors and the dragon slayer walked slowly around the caged three times but could not find an opening.

Finally, Zack sat down against some boulders. "I give up. You're right, Gruen, there's no way in or out of the cage."

They all turned at a noise from the tunnel. "Quick, over here," Tyler whispered, leaping behind some boulders. "I hope it's just Dell and Ellaby, but we have to be careful." They all huddled there watching the flickering light get brighter and brighter. Suddenly the light went out.

Out of the darkness, the two girls and Kittythwack appeared at the entrance, and Ellaby ran to her mother. Pottaby ran to Kittythwack and she licked his nose.

Dell stared at the cage and then at Doraby, who was hugging Ellaby through the bars. "This is most dreadful. How could anyone do something like this to someone as kind and sweet as Doraby? Calamar must be the most hideous of creatures."

They all came out from behind the boulders and Zack ran to Dell. He grabbed her arms. "Listen, we don't have much time. Was anybody in the tunnel?"

Dell shook her head. Tyler turned to Ellaby and asked, "What did Beadlesberry say?"

Ellaby turned her tear-stained face toward him. "He will call a town meeting for tomorrow morning at the lake. Ten o'clock sharp. He will tell everyone that Gruen has an announcement to make."

Tyler rubbed his hands together, "All right, it's coming together. Now if we can just figure a way to keep Doraby safe tonight, we'll be set."

Gruen said, "We must block the tunnel. Then Bramble and I will guard the cavern from the other entrance. I do not think the wizard has any power without his wand. Therefore, he will be unable to turn the beautiful Doraby into a dragon tonight."

"I just hope he doesn't have a spare wand," Zack muttered.

For the next hour, they all carried stones or rolled boulders to build a wall blocking the tunnel.

Bramble and Gruen grunted as they heaved the last of the boulders into place. "That should be sufficient to keep out even the most evil of wizards," Gruen said. Bramble nodded in agreement.

"I hope so," Doraby said softly. "I do not wish to become a dragon ever again."

"Oh mother," Ellaby said. "The brave warriors have a wonderful plan to trap the wizard tomorrow and they have stolen his wand."

"I never knew he was a wizard, Ellaby. He kept it a secret all this time," Doraby said.

"We could not believe it either, Mother. Everyone loves Calamar."

"Wait until tomorrow, then the whole town will know what he really is," Tyler said.

"Yes," Gruen added. "Tomorrow we thwart the Wizard of Maidenspa and free the dragon." Tyler felt a sharp pain in his stomach. He hoped their plan would work. So many things could go wrong between now and tomorrow morning. Then a giant hand pressed against his shoulder. "Do not distress yourself, young warrior, we shall prevail." Gruen looked down at him and smiled, his teeth pointing in every direction.

That night, the people of Balalac slept peacefully while Gruen and Bramble guarded the outside entrance. A low roar echoed through the tunnels when the Wizard found his way blocked by a solid wall of stone. Hiding behind the disappearing door in the Inn, the mighty warriors heard him invoke ten different versions of his name, but nothing happened.

They grinned in the dark. Calamar's power was now safely hidden in the trunk in Tyler's room, guarded by Pottaby. Without his wand, the Wizard of Maidenspa was helpless. Tomorrow they would unmask the Wizard to the entire town.

"'Night mighty warrior," Zack giggled, going into his room.

Tyler shook his head that suddenly felt too heavy for his neck. He didn't feel like a warrior, mighty or otherwise. He felt very tired. He wanted to be in his own room high above the streets of Manhattan. The silence scared him. He strained to hear sirens screaming and horns blaring, the city songs that put him to sleep every night. Tyler shivered as he curled up under the blanket, wishing the churning in his stomach would go away.

Chapter 19

Wizards, Dragons and Wands, Oh my!

Morning dawned sunny and peaceful, except for the rat-a-tat-tat of the woodpecker outside. Pottaby sat up on the trunk at the foot of the bed. "Good Pottaby," Tyler yawned, stretching. "You stayed there all night to guard the wand."

Pottaby woofed and jumped down, padding softly across the hall into Zack's room. "Yow, hey, get off my face," Zack yelled.

Tyler rolled off the bed, laughing. "He's better than an alarm clock."

"Shut up," Zack growled.

Tyler could hear Pottaby's paws clicking down the stairs. After using the bathroom, Tyler opened the trunk and took out the box with the wand. He pulled on his clothes and tucked the box in his pocket. "Hey, Zack, you ready yet?"

"I'm coming, I'm coming." Zack stuck his head in Tyler's door. "Man, this better work, cause I sure want to sleep in my own bed tonight."

"Yeah, me too," Tyler said. "I've had all I can stand of this world."

Zack nodded. "I mean, it's not like anybody's been mean or nasty to us. Well, maybe Beadlesberry for lying and everything. It's just…"

"Hurry young warriors. Crumble has pancakes for breakfast," Ellaby called.

The boys ran down the stairs. "You're happy this morning," Tyler said.

"Of course, brave warriors. I have found my mother and my father has returned. He is with her now in the cave. They are eating Crumble's pancakes together." Ellaby said, twirling around. "And, you, mighty warriors, have found the wizard."

"Okay. You did say pancakes?" Zack ran to the dining room right into Crumble. She pulled him into her arms and squeezed. "Oof." The air went out of him in a woosh.

"I am so happy, brave and mighty warriors. You have done a glorious deed for us." She let go of Zack to wipe a tear from her cheek and sniffle.

Zack staggered back, gasping. Tyler hid his grin behind his hand. Then Crumble turned toward him and Tyler backed away. "Uh, listen, Crumble, your fantastic pancakes are thanks enough."

Ellaby's giggle tinkled like wind chimes. "I think our brave young warriors know how thankful you are, Crumble, dear. Perhaps we should let them eat."

"She's right, Crumble, we know how grateful you are. Your delicious pancakes are enough thanks. Besides, we're starved after building the stone wall last night," Tyler said. Zack nodded.

"Of course, you must be exceedingly famished. What was I thinking? Come in at once and sit." Crumble bustled into the kitchen and returned with a huge platter of pancakes that towered precariously as she set it on the table.

"Eat, eat. There are popps to put on top. You must be strong for what is to come."

Tyler looked at the pancakes and a sour taste rose from his stomach. He suddenly wasn't hungry any more. Zack stuck his fork in the pancakes and speared five at once. Tyler watched him pour on the syrup and popps and slurp down the first bite. Nothing came between Zack and his stomach, Tyler thought. Out of the corner of his eye he could see Crumble waiting, expectantly. Taking a deep breath, he put three pancakes on his plate. He covered them with popps and took a bite. Okay, not too bad, like waffles and strawberries. His stomach settled down and before he knew it, three more pancakes had followed the first batch.

Crumble was very pleased. She smiled and went into the kitchen. Pottaby watched her disappear and crept under Tyler's chair to catch crumbs. Tyler slipped him an entire pancake and three popps. He could hear Pottaby happily sigh as the food disappeared into his tiny mouth.

"You will spoil him, Tyler Trent," Ellaby whispered, her tiny teeth gleaming.

Tyler shrugged and passed another pancake down to the floor. "He deserves it as much as we do. We couldn't have done it without him."

There was noise outside, the sound of voices and footsteps coming along the road. Ellaby looked up. "They are coming. I am frightened, Tyler Trent."

Tyler stood. “It’s gonna be okay, Ellaby. Don’t worry. Right Zack?”

Zack stuffed one more pancake and two popps in his mouth and nodded. Tyler took a deep breath to calm his stomach. It would be disgusting to barf up pancakes all over the dining room table now.

They all watched from the porch as everyone in town passed by and waved. There were shouts of surprise and delight when they saw the calm and peaceful lake. Beadlesberry stopped at the porch steps. “You have felled the dragon, young warriors, now you must deliver the wizard.” As he turned away, they could hear him cackling.

A few moments later, Dismar and his family came by with Calamar. The furious wizard glared at the trio on the porch. Zack leaned toward Tyler. “He knows.”

“He would probably turn us into griswallers if he had his wand,” Tyler whispered. Zack shivered. Tyler grinned. “Stop worrying, he doesn’t have the wand, I do.” Tyler patted his pocket just to make sure the box was still there. He was just as scared as Zack, but he wasn’t about to show it in front of Ellaby.

“Hello, brave warriors, Ellaby, Pottaby.” Dellthwack ran up the steps and hugged Ellaby. Then she knelt down and put her arms around Pottaby. The woofen licked her face. Kittythwack rubbed her body around Tyler’s legs and purred. He reached down and scratched her head.

“So, it is my understanding that you believed I was the wizard,” a deep voice boomed from the foot of the stairs.

Tyler stood up and opened his mouth. Before he could say anything, Ellaby rushed down the stairs and stared up at Drumthwack’s face. “Please forgive our brave warriors, Keeper of the Debts, they have no knowledge of anyone in Balalac. They could not have known of your kindness and generosity.”

“Humph, I suppose that is true. I am a most generous soul, brave warriors. I have forgiven many a debt to those who would pay if they could, but cannot.” Drumthwack nodded.

Tyler thought Drumthwack might just pat himself on the back in a minute. “We suspected a number of people, sir, before we made our decision,” Tyler said.

“Right, you weren’t the only one,” Zack added.

Drumthwack nodded and flipped his cape around him. “Yes, well, come along then and let us confront the Wizard of Maidenspa.”

Zack rolled his eyes. “Who’s us? Like he’s gonna do it,” he muttered.

Tyler said, "Yeah, well, it's now or never time, Zack."

"This better work," Zack said to himself. Tyler silently agreed, trying to keep down the pancakes.

They all followed the path to the lake and stood by the platform. Beadlesberry looked down on him and grinned wickedly, baring his teeth.

He gestured to the boys to join him on the platform. When they were standing beside him, he said, quietly, "People of Balalac." There was sudden silence as every head turned toward the platform. Tyler had barely heard him, yet it was so still he could hear the breeze rustling the leaves. He jumped as Beadlesberry said in a louder voice, "You see before you two valiant young warriors who have braved the elements of evil and solved the riddle of the boiling waters of Maidenspa."

There was a roar of applause. Beadlesberry held up his hand and the clapping stopped. This was like the concerts he attended with his parents at Lincoln Center. When the conductor brought his baton down, the entire orchestra stopped at once. Beadlesberry was speaking again. "Now I shall let brave Tyler Trent speak."

Tyler took a deep breath and stepped forward. He was sure everyone could see his knees shaking. Tyler cleared his throat, but only a squeek came out. Oh God, he thought, please don't let my voice start changing now. He tried again and his voice cracked. No, not now, please, God, not now.

Taking a deep breath, he said, "Um, we figured out what was happening. Um, why there was an earthquake every night, and why the lake was boiling in the morning. Uh, it has to do with Ellaby's mother, Doraby. It turns out there's a wizard who has imprisoned her in a cave under the ground. Every night he turns her into a dragon and it's the dragon trying to escape that causes the earthquakes."

Now he was on a roll. "The wizard put the cage over the underground stream that feeds the lake. Then when the dragon breathes fire it heats up the stream and makes the lake boil."

"That is hard to believe," someone said.

"Right you are. How do we know any of this is true?" a woman called.

A man in the back shouted, "Why would the wizard do this to Doraby. She would never hurt anyone."

Ellaby moved next to Tyler and put her hand on his arm. "Let me speak," she said. Tyler stepped back. Beadlesberry put up his hand and there was instant silence. Ellaby's soft voice could be heard across the field. "The wizard has masqueraded as one of us, someone we know and love."

There was a buzz and rustling as people looked around at their friends and neighbors. Beadlesberry once again raised his hand. Silence descended.

Ellaby continued, "The wizard was once in love with my mother, but she chose to marry my father, Dunby. He has kept his anger toward my parents inside for all this time, until he could stand it no longer. Then he exacted revenge in the most dreadful way possible, by hurting us all, especially my parents."

"So who is this wizard," Dismar called.

Beadlesberry stepped forward. "If you will all follow me, we shall go to where Gruen and Bramble are guarding Doraby, and there our valiant young warriors will unmask the Wizard of Maidenspa."

Tyler and Zack followed Beadlesberry down the stairs and around the lake. Tyler tried to find Calamar in the crowd, but lost sight of him. Gruen and Bramble were waiting at the entrance to the cavern and Bramble carried a wooden platform into the cavern. Beadlesberry climbed up onto the platform and watched as everyone crowded into the cavern and surrounded the cage where Doraby sat holding Dunby's hand through the bars. Esmara rushed over to Doraby and began to cry. Many of the women were crying and some men tried to surreptitiously wipe their eyes.

Tyler jumped on the platform and scanned the crowd for Calamar, finally spotting him hovering in the back of the crowd. Tyler spoke in Gruen's ear and the dragon hunter edged to the back of the cavern and stood silently behind Calamar. Bramble guarded the exit.

Beadlesberry raised his hand and all sounds stopped. When the echoes faded, Tyler said, "As you can see, everything we told you is true."

He pointed toward the walled entrance to the tunnels. "There is a series of tunnels underground, that the wizard used to visit Doraby each night and performed his magic transformation. We hid in there one night and watched him. We could not see who he was, but he used words that were anagrams of his name and in that way we were able to figure out who he was.

"Then we boarded up the tunnels with stones so he could not get through. Gruen and Bramble have been guarding the outside entrance. We figured he might not have any power without his wand, so Pottaby and I stole it from him."

The crowd murmured. Tyler continued. "Unfortunately, we still can't free Doraby, but at least the wizard can't turn her into a dragon. So it's a stand-off." He reached into his pocket and pulled out the box with the wand. He opened it and took out the wand, holding it up. "I challenge the wizard to show himself."

There wasn't any sound. People turned to look around at each other, wondering who among them might be the wizard. Tyler could see Calamar edging toward the opening, but Gruen stepped between him and the exit.

Then Tyler spoke, "So, Calamar, the Confectioner, don't you want your wand back?"

There was a gasp from the audience and everyone looked for Calamar. Gruen had one arm and Bramble had the other and they propelled him forward toward the platform. The crowd parted down the middle to let him through. The sound of everyone talking at once echoed off the cavern walls. The giants dragged him up on the platform. The noise was deafening. "Silence!" Beadlesberry roared, raising his hand. "I shall leave it to the people of Balalac to decide what we shall do with you, Wizard. If you value your life, you will follow brave Tyler Trent's instructions exactly or perhaps we will do away with you altogether."

People began to shout, "Evil!" "Wicked!" "Devil!" "Stone him!" "Boil him in oil!" "Drown him!" "Cut him up and feed him to the griswallers!" "Tie him to a tree, naked, and let the glowervogs eat him!" Everyone applauded the last idea.

Beadlesberry raised his hand and commanded silence. He turned to Calamar. "The people have spoken. Now you must make your choice."

Calamar pulled his black cloak around his body and stared down at the crowd. Then he turned and looked at Doraby. "I loved you, Doraby dearest. It was I you had chosen."

Doraby stood up holding the bars of the cage. Tears streamed down her face. "If you truly loved me, Calamar, you would not have hurt me in this way. Please release me from this prison."

Calamar watched her for a moment and then turned to Beadlesberry. "Very well, I do it for Doraby. Not because I fear the threats of these people." He looked with distain at the crowd and waved his arm as if to dismiss them. Calamar addressed Tyler. "So brave young warrior, what is it you would have me do?"

"You and Gruen will hold the wand together and you will say the words that will make the cage disappear. If you do anything else he will break the wand and probably your hand and arm, also," Tyler said.

Beadlesberry glared at Calamar. "If you try anything other than freeing Doraby, the entire town will descend upon you and destroy you by a most long and painful means."

Calamar shrugged. "If I do as you say, what happens to me?"

"Banishment," Beadlesberry said. The crowd grumbled. Angry words bounced off the walls. Beadlesberry held up his hand for silence.

"Hmm, very well. It appears that I have no choice," Calamar said.

Zack pulled Tyler's arm and said softly, "I don't know about this. He could say anything. What if he puts a spell on Gruen before Gruen can get the wand away?"

"I don't have any other ideas, do you?" Tyler said. Zack shrugged.

They giants dragged Calamar to the cage and Tyler followed with the wand. He handed the wand to Gruen. The dragon hunter held the wand in his left hand. With his right hand he took one of Calamar's hands and held it open. Calamar's entire hand disappeared into Gruen's enormous grip.

Everyone held their breath. "Say the words to open the cage," he growled. Gruen extended one of Calamar's fingers and touched it to the wand. Calamar grinned at Gruen and shouted "ALCOMAR."

Tyler almost shut his eyes, expecting to see Gruen turned into a toad. The cage disappeared. Calamar opened his mouth to shout something else, but Bramble clapped his enormous hand over Calamar's face. Gruen pulled back Calamar's hand and snapped the wand in half with one flick of his huge fingers. There was a gush of wind across the cavern as everybody let out a breath at the same time.

Doraby rushed into Dunby's arms and they both hugged Ellaby. Pottaby danced around woofing. Tyler reached out for the two pieces of broken wand and stuffed them back in the box. Everyone was clapping and shouting. Beadlesberry pushed through the crowd toward the opening with the giants right behind, nearly carrying Calamar between them. Tyler and Zack tried to follow but everyone wanted to thank them and clasp their hands or slap their back.

"Ouch," Zack exclaimed after one particularly hard slap on his shoulder. "I'm gonna be black and blue."

They finally got to the cavern exit and out into the fresh air. The boys collapsed under a tree, panting. "I can't believe we pulled it off," Tyler said.

"Man, for a minute there I thought it was all over," Zack said.

Tyler nodded. "When Calamar opened his mouth again, I thought we were all done for."

"Good thing Bramble was so fast." Zack said. "He could have turned everybody into griswallers."

"Or worse. We might have all been locked up in the cavern forever." Tyler held his stomach. "I knew I should never have had those pancakes."

"Don't you barf."

"Shut up, jerk."

"Up your...," Zack shut his mouth as Ellaby, Doraby, and Dunby cut off the sunlight.

The boys stood up. Doraby reached out and took their hands. "I cannot express my gratitude enough, young warriors. Your bravery and cunning saved us all." She sniffed and leaned against Dunby.

"How can we ever repay you, Tyler Trent and Zack Vander?" Dunby asked.

Zack grinned, "How about a swim in the lake?"

Everyone laughed. "You know you will never again be ill or hurt once you bathe in Maidenspa," Ellaby offered.

"My mother will never believe that," Tyler said.

"Mine either," Zack added.

"Does that mean my teeth will never get cavities, no matter how much candy I eat?" Tyler asked.

"You know what? I don't think I'll ever eat another piece of candy again," Zack said.

"Please, let us not speak of confection, dear brave warriors," Doraby said. "You will swim in the lake with Ellaby and her friends and then Crumble will prepare an enormous feast in honor of your wondrous achievement."

"Yes," Tyler said, taking Ellaby's hand. "Right now."

"Uh, Tyler." Zack grabbed his arm and pulled him away. "Home? Remember?"

"Sure I remember. I'm not an idiot. It can just wait a few more hours. Besides, we still haven't found the pendant," Tyler said.

"I have a funny feeling it's suddenly gonna show up," Zack said.

"Well, until it does, let's go swimming and eat. You still like to eat, right?"

Zack punched Tyler on the arm.

"Stop," Tyler shouted. "Stop!"

Everyone froze. "What is the matter, Tyler Trent," Ellaby asked.

Tyler waved his arms. "Look around. Does anything seem different?"

The small yellow polka-dot dog ran through the green grass. "Woof, woof," he barked.

Everyone grinned. "Pottaby says the happpiness is back," Ellaby shouted, twirling around in her multi-colored flowered dress.

Gone was the sad, dim world. Everything glowed with bright colors.

"You have brought us back to life again, Tyler Trent, brave warrior," Dunby said.

"And you, valiant Zack Vander. Thank you," Doraby said.

Chapter 20

The Way Home

Tyler had never felt so healthy in his life after a swim in the blue lake. Even the pain in his shoulders from all the pounding had disappeared. The meal was amazing, five different dishes. The boys didn't want to know what they were. They thought about their favorite foods like hot wings, lasagna, and sweet and sour pork with fried rice. Whatever they were eating tasted just like they imagined. The only person missing was Gruen, who had left, taking Calamar away with him. He said he would leave him with the first caravan heading to the icy north woods. Gruen assured them that the giant woodsmen would take very fine care of Calamar. Then he had to hurry off to Baldala where there had been a dragon sighting.

Dismar was too upset to join the festivities. He could not believe his cousin was a wizard. He assured everyone, "There has never been a wizard or a magician in our family. Perhaps he was switched at birth by a sorcerer. Yes, that must be the answer, switched at birth. Somewhere my own dear cousin Calamar is living another life. Oh dear, oh dear." Esmara dragged him away and put him to bed, after dosing him with his own herbs.

Drumthwack and Delthwacky attended the banquet. Crumble, after making a face and mumbling about purren hair all over the rugs, allowed Kittythwack to sit outside the dining room door with Pottaby. She gave them each a dish of treats. Ellaby smiled at Tyler behind her hand. He felt red heat rise up to the roots of his hair.

"You have been brave warriors, Tyler Trent and Zachary Vander. We are honored to have known you both," Dunby said solemnly. Doraby nodded, her dark eyes tearing. Dunby took her hand and rose. "Come dearest Doraby, you must rest after your ordeal."

Drumthwack stood. "I must go too. I have some debts to erase." He nodded at Zack and Tyler.

After they left, the four young people went outside on the porch. Tyler looked at the girls and announced, "You know, it's time for us to go home."

Ellaby looked down at her feet.

Ellaby raised her eyes to Tyler. "I hope you will never forget us, Tyler Trent."

"Me too," Dellthwacky said, smiling at Zack.

Zack brushed his hand over his face. "Um, I don't think we'll ever forget this adventure. Right Ty?"

"Never. I'll probably have night-, uh, dreams every night about dragons and wizards and yellow polka dot woofens and uh, you too," Tyler said.

Ellaby giggled and blushed; bright red this time. Pottaby rolled over and Zack rubbed his belly.

Kittythwack rubbed against Tyler's legs. Suddenly they heard the harsh cry of a raven. The large black bird settled on the porch railing. Pottaby jumped up and woofed. The raven dropped a shiny gold disk from its mouth, spread its huge wings and flew away. They could hear its cries fading into the distance.

"I knew it," Tyler shouted. "It was Beadlesberry all along." He lunged at the railing and grabbed the pendant. Tyler pulled out the black ribbon and strung the pendant on it. Then he put it around his neck and tucked it inside his shirt.

Zack breathed a huge sigh of relief. "I was really worried there man. I thought we'd never get it back."

Ellaby said, "You have found your lost pendant, Tyler Trent. I am happy for you. Now you can go home."

"Hey, maybe you'd like to walk us into town," Tyler said.

Zack looked at Tyler. "Yeah, we want to see Beadlesberry before we go."

"Of course, Zack Vander," Dellthwacky said.

They all trooped off down the road, waving goodbye to Crumble, who stood crying into her apron on the porch and Bramble towering over his tiny wife. When they reached town, the apothecary was closed and no one looked at the confectionary shop. They all stopped in front of the bookstore and said goodbye again.

Pottaby woofed. "He says have a safe journey," Ellaby translated.

Tyler bent down and patted Pottaby on his head. "Woof to you too." Hecould have sworn Pottaby grinned.

The boys entered the bookstore and the door clicked shut behind them.

Beadlesberry peered over the pile of books on his desk. "Aha, the brave young warriors, Tyler Trent and Zachary Vander."

Tyler wanted to drop some books on Beadlesberry's head, but maybe it was smarter just to go home. He pulled out the pendant and the boys grasped it in their hands. Tyler said, "Bookstore, reverse." Nothing happened. "Bookstore, reverse," he said louder. Nothing. The heavy metal band was beating a rhythm in his chest.

"What, what?" Zack yelled. "It's not working."

"I know that, Zack. Just shut up a minute so I can think."

"Okay, okay, just calm down. You must have said it wrong."

Tyler sat down and put his head in his hands. "Having problems, young man?" Beadlesberry stood over him.

Tyler looked up. "You know what's the matter, old man. It's not working."

"Yeah, we want to go home," Zack wailed.

"Try some wordsmithing, Tyler Trent," Beadlesberry said. "But make it fast, I have things to do and places to go." The bookshop started to shimmer.

What the hell was wordsmithing? Tyler jumped up. "Word play. Grab hold, Zack, this better work. Bookshop, reverse." Another flash of light and his tingling body was standing in the middle of the bookshop. Sunshine poured through the windows and he could see piles of dusty books. A car horn blared and sirens shrieked in the distance. Tyler ran to the window and looked out onto a New York City street. Sunlight glinted off the wet cars and pavement.

"We're back," Zack yelled, jumping up and down.

"So, boys did you have a good journey?" The old man stood behind them, a big grin on his face.

Words poured out of Tyler. "There was this dragon and a wizard and the raven stole the pendant. But you sent the raven or you were the raven."

Zack babbled, "I got stuck on a staircase to nowhere behind an invisible door. And the dogs and cats spoke their own language."

"Then when we saved Doraby, the raven returned the pendant but we couldn't return because I kept saying bookstore instead of bookshop…."

"Sit down, brave boys and have some lemonade. Just what you need after this adventure."

Tyler and Zack gulped the glasses of lemonade. They were very thirsty and suddenly very hungry. Beadlesberry seem to understand and handed them a plate of cookies. They ate them all.

His mouth still full of cookies, Tyler mumbled, "You hypnotized me, right. I mean, I didn't really go to Balalac, did I?"

"Of course you went there and back, brave Tyler Trent."

"It's impossible," Tyler said, shaking his head. "It can't physically happen."

"But it just did, my boy and you can do it again. You can go on many adventures."

"Uh, I don't know about that. I mean our families must be looking for us." Tyler started backing toward the door. "We really have to go now."

"Yeah, right. There must be a manhunt for us after a whole week," Zack said.

"Nonsense, my boy. You were only gone an hour," Beadlesberry said.

Tyler stopped. "What do you mean, an hour. We were there a week."

"There, but not here. Time is different in the Book of Mysteries." Beadlesberry's eyes gleamed.

"Why should I believe you? You lied to us," Tyler said.

"Did I now? I told you you would have a great adventure and would only be gone a few minutes. Is that not what happened, Tyler Trent?"

Tyler shrugged. "I guess so. But I said I wanted to go for only five minutes and now it's an hour."

Beadlesberry shrugged. "The adventure took a bit longer than I expected. Five minutes, 60 minutes, that is not important. You had a good time."

He lowered his eyes and glared at them. "You did have a good time, did you not?"

Tyler and Zack looked at each other. "I guess," Tyler said. Zack nodded.

"So there you are. Now give me the pendant and do come back. There are many more adventures in the Book of Mysteries. Oh, and Tyler, do give my regards to your father. He went to Egypt as I recall, or was it Mesopotamia?"

Dad too? Tyler wrenched open the door and the boys ran out into the street. They ran to the corner and turned around. Tyler could no longer see the wooden sign. He squinted into the sunlight and moved out into the street. The sign was gone. A car honked and Tyler jumped back up on the sidewalk. "The bookstore's gone, Zack. Doesn't anybody even notice?"

Zack shook his head. "Who cares. We got home.

It was almost 5 o'clock and if they didn't catch the next bus they would be late. How would they explain why they didn't make it home in time for dinner? He could just see their faces if he told them about the bookstore and wizards in the land of Balara. His mother would turn white and scream, "Not another Thaddeus." His father would just hide behind the New York Times and not say a word.

The bus came rumbling down the street. The boys pulled out their tokens and jumped on. As the bus started moving, Tyler felt something stab his side as he sat down.

He reached into his jacket pocket and pulled out a small wooden box with strange carvings on the lid. He gasped and looked out the window. The wooden sign, Beadlesberry's Rare Books, waved in the wind. The bookstore had reappeared. Tyler poked Zack and pointed at the sign. Then he raised his eyebrows and shrugged.

Zack folded his arms and shook his head. "No way, man," he muttered.

Tyler squeezed the box and grinned. "If you say so, Zack."

CPSIA information can be obtained at www.ICGtesting.com
Printed in the USA
238307LV00001B/7/P

9 780982 634424